MORNINGSTAR

This is a work of fiction. Similarities to real people, places, or events are entirely coincidental.

MORNINGSTAR

First edition. June 6, 2024.

Copyright © 2024 Tyler Moore.

ISBN: 979-8224578597

Written by Tyler Moore.

Dedication

I'd like to dedicate this novel to all the writers and artists in the world who wish to have their voices heard.
At the end of the day, our love for our craft is ultimately what we strive to feel complete in.
Complete, is what I hope you feel in my words and yours as well.
Often I find myself feeling fulfilled by being able to have this gift of story-telling. May you also feel fulfilled in your ways of the craft as well.

Prologue

I fell *down* with such force that the only noise that could be heard was my body falling through the sky. The clouds were moving all around me as I moved past them.

Shades of gray and black, a thunderstorm was instantly brewing. I could smell the thick rain that had started to form in the clouds.

"Father. Why?" I shouted towards the sky as I continued to fall.

I tried to flap my wings in despair, but nothing happened. The strength in my wings alone had disappeared almost altogether.

I had been cast out. Tears begin to form in the corner of my eyes and roll down the side of my cheeks.

"Forgive me!" I screamed towards the heavens.

Just then lightning passed through the sky and thunder crackled through the air echoing all around me. It was Dad.

"Just forgive me. I promise I didn't mean anything by it." I said while trying to navigate the air as I was tumbling from out of the sky.

It was too late for that. Lightning shot through my body, piercing my chest and burning my toes and fingertips. I felt the immense electricity burn and travel its way through my wings. The white coloring in my feathers was instantly changed to that of a black charcoal color. Feathers started to fall off of my backside and float into the air—one by one I watched as each one floated individually into the air as I continued my descent.

I was falling from grace.

MorningStar Chapter 1

I fell. I fell with a force so powerful the ground below me began to shake. I saw the impact coming. I was falling out of the sky so fast my wings were being torn to pieces. My black feathers began to flutter away in the wind. I never thought in a billion years, I'd be cast out. My love for him never stopped.

"I was his favorite." I thought.

But my thoughts, the whispers, they told me differently.

"Please forgive me, please forgive me, I'm sorry!" I screamed to the heavens, while still falling out of the sky.

Clouds begin to push past my eyes. I could feel it. I could feel the beating of my heart. Oh, how it ached, for forgiveness.

"Lord please have mercy on me!" I shouted.

The ground was rapidly approaching. I tried to summon up the strength to fly, but it was as if my powers had been ripped from me altogether.

Then, just like that. I impacted the ground. I struck the ground with such a fury, that the field around me was set ablaze.

SEVERAL HOURS LATER

I opened my eyes. I struggled to open them. Dirt covered my once beautiful face. I pushed myself up and studied the field around me. Wheat for miles, upon miles. I was confused as I looked down at my hands which were bruised and tattered. I had several cuts along my face and neck from falling out of the sky.

I collected myself to the best of my ability, as I shook the loose dirt out of my hair.

"Please, no. No. No. No." I cried.

"What am I to do now?" I screamed to the heavens, knowing he was "listening" as always.

I peered over my shoulders to look at my wings. The damage alone brought tears to my eyes. I was changing. I was becoming powerless. I spread out my wings and fell to the ground, on my knees. Tears formed in the corners of my eyes.

"All I've ever done is love you!" I screamed.

My voice echoed for what seemed like miles. I studied the ground for a moment. I picked up loose soil into my bloodied hands. Shifting it from one hand to the other.

"We built this together, you and I," I yelled.

The sun glistened off of my face as I felt the heat of it. It was beginning to set. The wind howled through me sharply as I felt it pierce my flesh for the first time. The cold. I felt the cold wind gust from the north and rush around me.

My tears rolled down my cheeks. I felt betrayed. I felt pure hatred.

"Curse you," I muttered under my breath.

"Curse you and all of the rest of my brothers and sisters," I said, raising my voice.

"Curse you for everything!" I screamed, now standing up with my fist towards the heavens.

"I'm done with you. Just like you are done with me!" I howled.

And, that was that. I got up and planted my feet into the soil. I felt rage pour through my heart. I was no longer full of love. I was full of hate. I walked. I walked away from it all. I walked away from him forever.

My name is **Lucifer Morningstar** *and this is my story.*

MorningStar Chapter 2

I wasn't sure where to begin. Or even, where to start. The important thing was I had been around for a while now. When I say that I mean it.

I've been around since the beginning of time. Let me show you...

Many millions of years ago my creator created the perfect world, the perfect galaxy, the perfect everything. Of course, there was somehow, one flaw in all of this, me. I was the flaw in his perfect design. Shit, right? That's what I said. Let's go straight to the source of it all, shall we?

Genesis 1:1- In the beginning, God created the heavens and the earth.

Hmm, God created the heavens and the earth. Pretty sweet design if you ask me. Then, I had some questions about free will and thought I was just a bit better, and bam! Cast out of Heaven just like that! I hit the Earth with such force all of the dinosaurs went extinct. None of them were alive anymore. *Look, you're welcome.* I did you all a favor. Who would want something from Jurassic Park tobe running around chasing tiny Tim down the street?

But I digress back to the big ol' book. This is where I come in.

Genesis 1:2-And the earth was without form, and void; and darkness was upon the face of the deep. And the Spirit of God moved upon the face of the waters.

Yep. I flooded the earth. We both did in fact. Only, when I did it, everything was wiped out. All those little fossils you find here and there on your little digs are from yours truly. I guess you have me to thank for all of your museums.

At any rate, this is how things came to be. Two floods. One from being cast down out of the heavens and the other from him just wanting to flood the earth entirely. But, he did however promise he wouldn't do it again. Rainbows, and all of that.

"SO THAT'S THE STORY, ladies and gentlemen," I said in my drunken state as I took a sip of my whiskey and took a hit off of my cigar at the bar.

"That's the story of how I, Lucifer Morningstar, flooded the world." I chuckled.

The bartender cautiously watched me for a moment before taking the whiskey glass from me.

"You're cut off." Said the bartender to me.

His voice was deep and raspy. It scratched against my ears. Most human voices did this when they were impure.

"Yeah, I wouldn't do that if I were you." I stared at him while locking eyes.

The thing about an immortal fallen angel is it still had its perks. I could still have my way if I concentrated hard enough. After millions of years of walking the earth, I had figured out how to manipulate humans, if I wanted to.

"I'm-. I'm sorry bout that." Replied the bartender to me as if he was in a trance.

"Don't worry about it, kid. Your sins are forgiven, if you just ask." I said, before winking at him.

The rest of the bar had quickly turned away from my story. Also, the fact I had just tranced the bartender. Nobody was paying attention at this point. I knew the story would go way over their heads. Most mortals had always just turned a blind eye to me. I was used to it.

The bartender started cleaning up the rest of the bar. But, I wanted another shot of this honey whiskey.

I whispered a thought into the mind of the bartender.

"You will pour me another shot," I whispered.

"This one's on me." He said while staring at me like a statue, that was barely able to speak.

"Of course it is," I said drinking the shot and slamming down the glass.

I took a drag off my cigar before adjusting my black peacoat and getting up from the barstool. My time here was done. I walked out of the bar and onto the busy streets of the town of Nashville. Something wasn't quite right. I could feel it, deep within me. I wasn't sure if it was a combination of the cigars and whiskey, or something else.

Morningstar Chapter 3

I did what I did best. I hid. I hid from everybody. I even hid from Dad. It didn't take long to get out of the city limits of Memphis. I realized my feathers were beginning to drop to the ground slowly as I came down to the ground. I spread my wings proudly looking over my shoulder to my right, and then doing the same for the left wing. The midnight sky was peaceful.

I was losing my abilities. I was dying. I couldn't help it. Nobody could. All I could do now was accept my fate. Just like I accepted, being kicked out of the heavens all those thousands of years ago.

"Some things just really aren't made to last forever," I said while flipping the bird up to the skies.

I still had a slight buzz from the honey whiskey from the bar.

I balled up my fists and slammed them into the cold hard ground.. I felt the pain in my knuckles climb up my wrist.

I was experiencing a shift.

A shift is when an immortal becomes a mortal. It's hard to explain, really. But I, Lucifer Morningstar, was shifting. Shifting fast. The next stage after this would surely kill me. This vessel had been around for thousands of years. I had controlled it since the very beginning of creation.

"From dust we come and dust we shall return," I said up towards the sky.

I fell to my knees, lighting up my cigar that I had from my pocket, and I took a big hit in. I held the smoke in my lungs for several seconds before exhaling. My breathing was becoming rapid. The shifting would soon be complete.

"Why? Why put me as a flaw in your perfect design and then cast me aside like some worthless piece of trash!" I shouted.

I had tears beginning to form in my eyes. My vision was blurry. I was fading.

"Father," I said while wiping my tears away.

"Forgive me," I said under my breath.

I meant it. Every word of it. Just then the clouds parted and the full moon shined brightly in my direction. A light from above was coming down to me at full force. It looked as if it was going to hit me. I quickly got off my knees and started to back up slowly.

The light wasn't slowing down. It looked like a meteor. A shooting star from the heavens. It could be only one thing.

"Gabriel," I said with a smile.

My brother.

Morningstar Chapter 4

I wasn't sure what to make out of it. I just knew it was Gabriel. He was coming down hard, and fast from out of the sky. Something wasn't right. I hadn't seen him since the dark ages. Then just like that, he touched down swiftly. It wasn't an impact like mine. It's as if a feather had fallen out of the sky onto the ground.

His back was turned to me as he landed by the cliffside, overseeing the flowing river. Night had turned to day in the blink of an eye when he touched down. The sun was well beyond the horizon now. An overcast filled the skies. All was quiet. All was still. He fell to his knees and looked down over the waters. His hands were extended outwards. He was praying.

"Gabriel?" I said.

"Yes, my brother?" He replied quietly.

His back was still turned to me.

"Did he send you?" I asked, my voice beginning to shake.

I was fading still. My immortalness was leaving my body and the vessel was quickly becoming useless.

"Yes. Yes, He sent me." His voice was now louder to where I could hear it more clearly.

"Does that... Does that mean that—-" I said before being interrupted.

"Yes. It's precisely what it means." He said, now standing up tall and proud.

His wings were much more defined. You wouldn't think his feathers to be, gray, but they were. The colors almost reminded me of ash, left over from a campfire.

"But, I don't want to fight you, brother," I said with my voice shaking.

"Dad's orders. An order is an order." Said Gabriel now facing me.

His face had its flaws. For he had seen great battles over thousands of years. Both spiritually and in the mortal realm of Earth. As for Gabriel and I, we had never fought before. But, I knewwith the condition I was in, I would quickly perish.

"You don't have to do this," I said taking a step towards him.

"He's restoring your powers." Said Gabriel, quickly.

He was receiving messages from the heavens.

"He's what? But why?" I asked.

Gabriel took two steps towards me in my direction.

"Because he's testing me in battle." Said Gabriel now with a motionless face.

You could tell he was getting tired of the back and forth.

"So, wait a minute. This asshole wants me to fight you at full strength, just so he can test you in battle?!" I shouted.

Gabriel nodded.

"Dad heard you ask for forgiveness. If you beat me in battle, you'll be able to keep the vessel. But if I beat you... Well when I beat you, you'll take your final breath". Gabriel said now smiling ever so slightly.

I was conflicted. All I wanted was to walk amongst my brothers again. I didn't want to fight my brother.

"This is stupid brother. Can't you see the games he plays us at?!" I shouted now just a few steps from Gabriel.

His fists were clenched.

Then as quickly as it was going to begin, it ended.

"I know, Lucifer." He said smiling and then shrugging slightly.

He took three steps backward toward the edge of the cliff.

"That's why you win." He said now quiet again.

The waters from below were roaring. The sky was fogged over still. And, just like that he was gone. With one quick motion, he threw himself backward off of the cliff and into the roaring waters, never to be seen again.

"No!" I screamed while running towards the edge and looking over.

My strength was returning. My black wings were stretched out as I studied the waters looking for Gabriel. I could feel his life force fading. He was no longer with me.

The real battle was only beginning. I had to find answers to what was going on.

I had to find Michael. I leaped off the cliff and flew away from the roaring waters into the rising sunrise. I was furious. I was going to find out what was going on, one way or another.

MorningStar Chapter 5

I was beyond angry. I flapped my wings furiously. I was still headed toward the rising sun. I knew if I followed this path, eventually, I would end up in Michael's vicinity.

"Gabriel. My poor brother. Why would you do that?" I thought out loud while flying higher into the clouds.

I was nearly above the clouds at this point. I knew the answer. He had sacrificed himself so I could be made whole again. I felt my strength returning. My powers were coming back to me. Everything was as it had always been.

"I'm sorry my brother, I won't let your death be in vain," I said now gliding above the clouds.

My wings had returned to their beautiful glossy black color. Feathers that were missing had miraculously grown back.

"Why continue to test me? If I'm such a burden in your grand design, why would you put me through so much? All I ever wanted to do was to help. Am I so wrong that I thought I could make it better!" I screamed, knowing Father was listening.

If I found Michael he would know what to do. He had the ability to even save Gabriel. Michael's role as an archangel was simple, really. Michael was the angel of death. Carrying the souls of all the deceased to heaven was his real job. In the hour of death, he gave the soul the chance to redeem itself before passing. All I had to do at this point was find exactly where he was. He was also in charge of all the other angels. He should have been there when Gabriel threw himself off the cliff into the waters. I had to have answers. Something wasn't adding up right. Something I couldn't quite place my finger on.

I was nearing my threshold. I was flying so fast at this point, that even the clouds were flashing by my line of sight. In the reality of things when I did find Michael, it wouldn't be a pleasant visit. No. His love for Him was far too great, to be happy to even remotely see me. I knew what I had to do in order to find him. I had to pray. I began to descend. Past the clouds, into an open field. The fog had cleared up and the sun was high in the sky. No mortals were around; which was something we always looked for before walking the earth. *You couldn't really explain that you just saw a man with black feathered wings touch down in the middle of a field, now could you?*

My feet planted firmly on the ground. . All around me was corn stalks reaching towards the skies. Luckily, I didn't leave any crop circles this go around. Yes, when angels touch down on earth, normally, they leave their signs. It started a big thing back in the seventies and eighties. Mortals were blaming it on little green men, in flying saucers. "Unexplained" they called it. I used to touch down purposely in corn fields, leaving signs, just to get a rise out of the locals in the area. But, enough about that.

The green stalks surrounded me for miles. A nearby irrigator was watering the cornfield. You could hear the ticking of the water, spraying out of the irrigator, repeating the same mechanical noise over and over.

I fell to my knees. The dirt rolled over my knees and hands. I clinched the dirt into the palms of my hands, and let the excess dirt roll off of my palms.

I extended my hands and began to pray.

"Saint Michael the Archangel, defend us in battle. Be our protection against the wickedness and snares of the devil; May God rebuke him, we humbly pray; And do thou, O Prince of the Heavenly Host, make yourself appear before me, as I humbly ask for your protection and guidance." I said out loud with my eyes closed.

The ticking of the irrigator stopped. The wind changed directions all around me. Instead of it flowing in one general direction, it spiraled in multiple directions before coming to a complete stop altogether. I listened for noise. No noise could be heard. The wind, the wildlife, and the ambiance of any noise were completely gone. The fluttering of heavy wings could be heard from above. I looked up towards the sky in the direction of where I heard the fluttering. I was still kneeling down on the ground. I cocked my head to the right and then the left to look behind me. Majestic white feathered wings, were now planted onto the ground behind me. A face was staring directly at my backside. The loose soil felt cold to the touch as I got up and slowly turned around. The white wings were folded out still from shoulder to shoulder.

It was Michael.

MorningStar Chapter Six

"Michael," I said without hesitation. His wings were still pointed up towards the sky. He glared at me. His fist were clenched.

"Lucifer." He said before exhaling a big breath.

"What did you do?" He asked taking big steps towards me.

"Michael, there's no time to explain, I need you to help. Gabriel…" I said, in a panic.

It was already too late. His fist was in a ball, ready to strike and that's precisely what he did when he was within arm's length. I got hit with such force on my jawbone that the very ground shook. A small fracture line in the dirt appeared as I fell to the ground. My eyes closed shut as I tried to focus. I was down on the ground. I started to push myself back up and was struck again by Michael. This time he grunted as he hit me across the back of my head. Down in the dirt I went, eating a mouth full, as I impacted the soil.

The irrigator had started back up. It was right above us. The ticking mechanism noise faded in and out, as Michael continued to repeatedly hit me. Only an angel could make another angel bleed. Blood had started to trickle from my forehead and brow, blinding my vision in my right eye.

"Wait, brother. I need you to listen." I said, with blood now forming around the corners of my mouth.

"You bastard." Said Michael, hitting me over the head again.

"You killed him." He said, lifting me and throwing my body against the irrigator..

I could feel my blood pulsating. A ringing in my ears started, it felt as if my body had been hit by a freight train, as I fell back to the ground.

My eyes were beginning to roll in the back of my head. Everything was starting to get blurry. He wasn't going to stop. Not until I was dead. In the reality of things, Father must have been permitting it, otherwise, Michael wouldn't have been allowed to beat me down to such a condition.

I was feeling my life force being drained. But the rage. The thousands of years of rage were coming forward. I could feel it course through my veins. I was becoming angry. Filled with it, so much so, that I was done with Michael's games.

"You need to list—" I tried to get out before being hit, again.

"I didn't hurt Gab—-" I said, being hit again over the top of my head with such force, that the ground cracked all around us.

"Goodbye, Lucifer." He said as he drew back his arm towards the sky while holding my head in his other hand.

He was going to hit me with a fatal blow. As his fist approached my head, I dug deep into the ground. Right before the impact, I shielded myself with my wings in front of my face. Then just like that a sonic boom happened as his fist connected with my wings. He tumbled backward through the cornfield, as I slid ever so slightly in the dirt backward still in the kneeling position I was in. I stood to my feet.

"Michael, I swear. You're just as hard-headed as Dad is." I said while cracking my neck from side to side.

He quickly got up, tossing the corn stalks to the side of him, away from him. He was pissed. I didn't care. I needed him to calm down. I needed him to understand.

"Don't do this." I yelled in his direction.

The wind started to pick up and spiral in circles. The cornstalks started slapping me ever so slightly across my arms and face.

"I'm doing this for Gabriel." Shouted Michael back at me, while full-on sprinting towards me.

"Have it your way." I said angrily.

I was now in a full-on sprint towards Michael. He started to hover off the ground with his wings before impacting me. I went in for a blow and connected with his jawline with my right fist. He quickly fell to the ground. He skidded backward, tumbling as he went back into the cornstalks. The irrigator was dripping water on us.Cool, brisk, water mixed with my blood on my brow and dripped onto my cheek, before falling off my chin onto the dirt. Michael was standing again, marching towards me, pushing the stalks out from in front of him. His wings fluttered as he arched them in such a way, that his wings connected with the cornstalks on his left and right side of him.

"I didn't kill him," I said. My voice echoed for miles in all directions.

"Can't you see it, brother? The madness of it all." I shouted at him.

"You should be in Hell, Lucifer. Where you belong." He said, spitting blood from out of his mouth, onto the ground.

He wasn't listening to what I was trying to say. I had to get through to him some way or another.

"Gabriel threw himself off the cliff into the damn water. You need to go do your damn job, instead of fighting with me and save his soul. There's only so much time to help him ascend." I said trying to reason with him.

He stopped. He stopped moving altogether. His composure completely changed. He bowed his head and lowered his wings.

"This isn't over Lucifer. I'll do what Dad is asking of me, but not because you asked me." Said Michael, now un-clenching his fist.

He took in a deep breath and exhaled.

"I'll make sure Gabriel ascends. As for you, consider this a warning. Should my path ever cross yours again, or should you find yourself praying to me again, I will kill you." He said now spreading his wings out.

"Yeah, yeah I've heard it all before, from the whole lot of you." I said mildly, chuckling under my breath.

His eyes appeared hollow staring back at me. He wasn't pleased with my comment. I didn't care. He needed to go find Gabriel's physical form and return him to Heaven. I wasn't sure about how the process exactly worked other than Michael was the caretaker of the dead. He made sure souls had the opportunity to ascend to Heaven. Regardless of Gabriel's sin of self-sacrifice, I'm sure the judging process of his soul would be overlooked. Gabriel was too important to Dad. Understand that his sacrifice restored my strength and powers. Without him, I would have perished.

Blood trickled down the side of Michael's mouth. His wings were still spread outwards. He shook his head from left to right while making a stern face in my direction.

Then just as he was there, he was gone. He pushed his wings in a downward motion, levitating for a moment before shooting up toward the sky. I lost sight of him a few seconds later. I stood idly in the cornfield before coming back to my senses. The rage was leaving my body.

Michael would find Gabriel and return him home. In the end that's all I wanted. I wanted to make sure Gabriel was okay. After all, he was my favorite brother, next to Raphael. I still needed answers though. I needed to make my way back into the city. Back to Nashville. I needed to go to the church.

MorningStar Chapter 7

I was still recovering from the fight with Michael. He got me pretty good back in the cornfield. It wasn't my first tussle with him. We had fought several times before, but not like this. He had rage in his eyes when he hit me repeatedly. The main thing I could gain from all of this was the fact that he got to Gabriel in time. You see, upon the hour of death of a soul, Michael had to be there in time to help that soul ascend to Heaven. Time wasn't relative to angels. Michael could almost completely stop time to take care of one soul during the hour of death. That way he could cover all the souls of the Earth that needed to be ascended.

I twitched my right eye closed and squinted briefly. A sharp pain could be felt on my brow from where Michael had struck me. The beauty of it all was that I healed relatively fast. I had already found a change of clothes and I was headed into the city of Nashville, the year was 2023. The mortal world was in chaos. Faith was scattered among the masses of churches and there were denominations upon denominations. Everybody had their interpretation of the "Big Book." They also had their interpretation of us, Angels.

I flew as close to the city as I could get, while still staying out of sight of any mortals. This was one rule I was bound to. Should I break it, or be deemed that my actions were disrupting the natural flow of mortals, Dad would cut me down to nothing. I'd be turned to dust in an instant. This was the one rule that I followed. I mean come on, could you imagine a world without me? I touched down by a nearby Casey's gas station on the outskirts of town. It was relatively quiet for the most part. Nobody saw me land behind the back of the building. I was thirsty. One thing that got me going more than anything else was caffeine. The nectar of the Gods, I called it. Just my luck, I had no money. Michael must have knocked my wallet out of my back pocket. Good thing I was persuasive. My shirt was tattered with blood stains that I had put on to hide my wings. I could hide my wings by retracting them into my body. Not all the way, but just enough that I appeared to be an average Joe.

I entered the Casey's General Store in search of my next caffeinated beverage.

"Welcome to Casey's." Said the gas station attendant.

I didn't say anything back. I didn't care about being polite at this point. It wasn't necessarily in the right mindset for mannerisms. See, caffeine speeds up the healing process. Not only was it anti-inflammatory for mortals, it had healing factors for us angels, and I needed a lot of it.

I got what I needed. One giant cup of hot coffee, and five energy drinks. I sat them down at the counter where the gas station attendant was. My hands were full and I had them stacked up on my arm. One by one I sat them down on the counter, starting with the coffee. I could tell she was questioning why I had so many. One by one she rang them up.

"Your total will be $18.67." She said, still looking at the energy drinks and coffee, and then back at me.

I read her name tag while slowly grinning.

"Zoey is it," I said, still smiling.

"Yes. Your total is $18.67." Said Zoey.

She wasn't having it. I had to dig deep with my charms. Luckily for me, I was very persuasive.

"Zoey you see I have no money," I said, still grinning at her.

Her blank stare told me that she didn't care.

"But, I'll tell you what Zoey. I'm in a good mood. I also have very little time and I got a killer headache." I said while leaning against the counter and putting my palms together.

"Look man, if you can't pay, I can't serve you. Store policy." She said now aggravated.

"Ooh, Feisty are we. Zoey listen to me very carefully." I said while making direct eye contact with her. Her eyes were now locked on mine.

"You're going to let me walk out of here without paying. Because to be honest, you've stolen before, haven't you? The donuts, the coffee, the Mountain Dew's at the end of the day from the store, haven't you?" I said.

"Ye-. Yes, I have." She said now in a trance. She was under my complete control.

"I understand. I'm going to walk out the door now, Zoey." I said while grabbing my coffee and taking a nice long sip.

"You're going to walk out now." She said.

"Can I have a sack please?" I asked Zoey.

She reached below the counter pulled out a sack, and started packing up my five energy drinks.

"Here you go, sir." Said Zoey now perfectly still, almost speaking in a monotone voice.

"Thank you, Zoey," I said while grabbing a pair of black lense sunglasses that were for sale by the counter.

"I'll be taking these also," I said tapping the left corner of the sunglasses that were now on my face.

"You'll be taking those also." Said Zoey, still speaking in a monotone voice.

I walked out of the store, feeling good about myself. A little persuasion goes a long way with mortals. No, they weren't bound for hell or anything like that. That was up to Dad. Not I. I had no control over that, whatsoever. I downed my coffee, the scorching heat running down my throat.

"Mmm, French vanilla," I said.

I quickly threw the coffee cup to the wayside. The heat from the sun was now coming down on me. I cracked open one of the energy drinks and downed it within seconds, throwing it to the side as well. What? You didn't expect me to be perfect did you? After all, I was the "Father of Lies" The original, the very first. Sure, there was a trash can right to the left of me, but I wasn't going to pick up my trash. I let out a big yawn, stretched, and cracked open another energy drink. This time I sat it down on the ground and proceeded to open up a second one. I picked the one up off the ground and had one in each hand. I could feel myself being rejuvenated. The part of my face that had been impacted and bloodied over was completely healed. I drank both of the energy drinks at the same time. Opening my mouth wide, so all the liquid traveled down my throat quickly. I shrugged my shoulders, feeling my wings tingle slightly. I was good to go.

The rest I would drink later. I needed a ride. Too many mortals were around to fly. I needed to get to the church.

Luckily for me, I knew a girl that was giving out free coffee and energy drinks, that wouldn't mind if I borrowed her ride.

MorningStar Chapter 8

The radio was playing. "Sympathy for the Devil" by the Rolling Stones. I was cruising down the highway with the top down. It was a blacked-out 1969 Charger, with all the bells and whistles. Apparently, Zoey's boyfriend had good taste. He had let her drive it to work. He wouldn't be missing it. Although, I did feel bad for Zoey. No, you're right. I didn't feel bad.

I felt the wind blow through my thick hair, I was nearing ninety-five miles an hour. The license plate on the Charger said, "Vroom". I was really pressing down on the accelerator. I adjusted the sunglasses I had picked up at Casey's gas station and took a swig off my energy drink.

"Mmm," I said as I downed the last bit of the drink.

I threw the can out onto the highway. I looked in the rearview mirror as it tumbled out onto the road. I weaved in between traffic. Passing trucks and cars cutting them off in the process. I felt the engine vibrate the entire car. The exhaust was loud, but the music through the radio was louder. I was having way too much fun with this car. I was nearing my exit. I got into the right-hand lane and exited the highway. The last little bit of "Sympathy for the Devil" was playing through the radio.

"Your classic rock station, Nashville's finest 104.7 The Throttle, will be right back after these important messages." Said the DJ through the radio.

I turned off the radio. I couldn't stand commercials or news. They irritated my blackened soul. I was just about at the church. One more left turn and I'd be there. But, wait a second, why exactly are we going to a church you ask? Patience people. I haven't even gotten to the good part.

There was the church, just as it had always been there. My lucky day, it was Sunday. Church was in session. The lettering on the church sign read: "If God is real so is the devil, rebuke Him!"

This was going to be fun. You see, I had a friend in this church. A very old friend that owed me something for eternity. Something he thought was trivial. He made a deal with me. A church for a soul. I did a little persuading with building the Pastor's church. He needed money, I got him money. He needed people to fill the church pews, I got him just that. The time on the radio read 10:20 am. The church sign said church services 10:00-11:30 am. I was just in time for the best part. The sermon. I found a parking spot out on the east side of the church parking lot. It was filled with cars. Attendance was booming. As it had always been since I made my deal with Pastor John. I called him PJ for short. He didn't like it when I visited. But a deal was a deal. I had questions that needed to be answered and PJ might just have the answers.

I killed the engine. Jumping over the door and onto the gravel of the church parking lot. I studied my face for a moment in the driver's side mirror of my newly acquired ride. I slicked back my hair, looking at my reflection. Appearance was everything. Especially when it came to seeing an old friend. I shook my shoulders from left to right, slowly making an adjustment to my wings. The more I shook the more my feathers seemed to be relieved. They didn't like being confined or retracted.

I opened my last energy drink. Sipping on the sweet nectar. I casually skipped up to the front steps of the church and did a complete three-sixty. I was feeling good. My luck was in my favor.

"Give em a good show," I muttered to myself out loud.

I was pumping myself up before entering the church. My black suit coat had a little bit of dust on it. Probably from going so fast down the highway. Then just like that, I opened the gigantic front doors to the church. The creaking of the door echoed from the inside out. Light poured in from behind me into the congregation hall. The pews were full of people. Heads turned as I entered. An elderly man from behind the pulpit shielded his eyes from the light that had poured in from outside when I entered the church. All eyes were on me. I pointed finger guns, in the direction of the man up on the stage, firing them as I made my approach. All was silent. Then the voice came from the stage from the elderly man. I knew who it was. It was Pastor John.

He tried to ignore the fact that I was standing in the middle of his pews halfway to the stage.

"As I was saying brothers and sisters, the devil is alive and real! He comes like a thief in the night! All he needs to do is get his foot in the door." Said Pastor John.

"Yeah yeah yeah," I said abruptly, cutting him off.

He tried to ignore me again. This time speaking louder.

"*1 Peter 5:8, says, Be sober-minded; be watchful. Your adversary the devil prowls around like a roaring lion, seeking someone to devour.*" Said Pastor John now in a panic knowing it was me.

I took a few more steps toward the stage. Pastor John, made a notion to a few people out in the congregation. The deacons of the church stood up. They weren't having it. They started to make their way toward me.

"PJ, you just never learn do you?" I said in his direction while snapping my fingers on my right hand.

That was all it took. The deacons that were coming my way instantly froze. In fact, everything and everyone froze except, Pastor John.

He was frantically backing away from the stage steps as I walked up them. The clocks stood still. The only movement was from John.

"PJ! How the bloody hell are you?" I asked while grinning.

"Get back! I rebuke you in the name of the—-" Said John before being interrupted by me.

"Just stop this PJ, I don't have time for this," I said, rubbing my forehead.

"I just have one question for you. Then you can have your precious soul back and keep your church. " I said holding up one finger in his direction.

His mouth was shut. That got his attention.

"Where is my brother Raphael?" I said with a stern face.

Morningstar Chapter 9

"How should I know where he is?" Said John looking at his frozen-in-place congregation.

The reason for asking him about Raphael is because of the deal he had made with me. Right after my little visit with John, Raphael came into the picture. He warned John of what he had done and how to protect and rid himself of any demonic presence. Raphael is said to guard pilgrims on their journeys also.

Not a single soul was moving. Everything was at a standstill. Just one of many tricks I had up my sleeve. I wasn't the least bit worried about the consequences either. I'd deal with that later. I had questions that needed to be answered. I needed to know why Gabriel was sent to fight me. I needed to know why I had started to shift after I had left the bar. Raphael could help answer some of my questions.

"John, I'll make this simple for you. You either tell me where my brother is, or so help me. I'll devour your soul right here, right now." I said while snarling my teeth.

My eyes went from a shade of blue to a shade of red, while making eye contact with John.

"Please no!" He shouted so loud his voice echoed through the church.

Sunlight was pouring in through the stained glass windows, shining on all the church members who were still frozen.

"Back you demon. Back Beelzebub. I repent you". Screamed John.

I was growing tired of these games.

"John. Listen to me," I said while glaring into his eyes. I demanded he listened.

"I'm listening to you." He said, now under my control. He was also frozen like the rest of the people in the church.

"I need you to tell me if you know where Raphael is," I said as seriously as I could.

"Raphael." He said smiling.

"The angel of healing." Said John still smiling.

"Yes, tell me where he is," I said abruptly.

I could feel a presence in the church that didn't quite belong. Something otherworldly. Someone who wasn't human.

"He's right behind you." He said.

He was mystified by whatever he was looking at now behind me.

I looked over my left shoulder, I could see the outline of six wings and a figure.

"Lucifer MorningStar." Said Raphael, his voice echoing throughout the church.

I turned around now facing my brother Raphael. I threw my hands up and back down to my sides. I was happy to see him. His wings were majestic not only did he have a pair above his shoulders. He also had a pair coming out from around the middle of his back as he did down by his hips. They dragged along the floor of the church. His feathers were as white as snow on a mountaintop. His eyes were a shade of blue like the tropics of the ocean water. He was magnificent.

"You've been busy I see. Dad will not be happy with this." He said while staring at the floor while shaking his head back and forth.

The light glistened off of his feathers and a small point of light shined above his brow. I respected Raphael. He and I did not quarrel in the past. The only thing I didn't like was him finding wiggle room in my affairs with mortals. John was speechless. Seeing Raphael in his spiritual form would have killed him. The best Raphael could do is appear in this form to the both of us. The rest of the people in the congregation were still standing still. John was in a trance, but not because of me anymore. He was in a trance because of Raphael's form. Father must have allowed it, otherwise he wouldn't have been able to be present.

"I've been looking for you brother," I said, taking steps off the stage into the middle of the pews where Raphael was.

His wings casually touched the nearby deacons of the church that were on his left and right.

"Come. You have questions and I have answers." Said Raphael now turning his back to me and taking small steps away from both John and I.

"Leave the mortal alone. You got what you wanted, I'm here now." Said Raphael his voice still booming and echoing throughout the church.

My brothers were of few words. They didn't talk much. In fact, one word in angelic tongue was the equivalent of a thousand mortal words. I turned back to John who was still in awe of Raphael's form.

We made our way to the basement of the church that was lit with candles on opposing sides. The candlelight flickered off of the walls and shadows of various objects. The light showed no shadow for Raphael. As for me, my shadow showed what appeared to be a normal mortal's shadow. Nothing majestic about my shadow in this form. We took the rounding steps down into the basement. It was full of tables and a kitchen. I followed his lead. He stepped gracefully with each step that he took.

"I'm sure you're wondering why I'm here." Said Raphael now looking at the ground.

He had stopped moving altogether. The only movement he had made was to turn around and face me.

"I actually came–" I said before being interrupted by my brother.

"Came looking for me. I know Lucifer." He said gracefully.

"What are your questions?" He said.

"Well, if you are going to say what I'm saying before I say it, why would I even say it?" I said mildly, chuckling.

"Fine. I promise not to do it. Ask your questions." He said while making eye contact with me.

I paused for a second, wondering exactly what I was going to ask, then it came to me.

I rubbed my face and eyes while stretching out my shoulders because my wings had been confined for so long. Normally this wouldn't have bothered me, but after my fight with Michael, I was still mildly sore.

"First off. I need to know if Gabriel is okay. I need to know that he ascended." I said in a serious tone.

"Second I want to know why Father sent him to fight me and I had started to shift moments before his arrival." I said.

Raphael pondered the questions for a few seconds before answering.

He took his hands and raised them up above his shoulders. He was praying. Communicating with the other angels and Dad.

This was something I lacked. When I fell from grace, Dad had made it impossible to communicate with my brothers and him. He dropped his hands to his sides and began to smile in my direction.

"Yes. Gabriel has ascended. He's with father now." Said Raphael in an excited tone.

He was just as happy as I was to receive such good news.

"You really didn't harm him did you?" Asked Raphael.

"I wouldn't harm him even if asked to," I said, curious as to why my brother just asked me that.

"Wait, you thought I killed him?" I asked in a worrisome tone.

He didn't answer. He just stared at me with a blank look. The same look Gabriel had given me, moments before he threw himself off the cliff.

"As for your second question. You are being tested. Tested for what purpose is unknown to me. I do not have the answers that you seek" Said Raphael.

His wings shuffled. He was in a mild panic. I wasn't sure why.

"All I can tell you is that you must return to the Garden." He said nervously.

I was confused. I hadn't stepped foot in the Garden since I had convinced Eve to eat the forbidden fruit from the Tree of Knowledge.

I was choked up.

"Why?" I said, staring at my brother.

Raphael's stare was emotionless.

"Because you must—". He said before stopping.

"Because you must take the fruit from the tree of knowledge and–," Said Raphael.

"And what?" I asked, grabbing my brother by his hands.

"You must eat from the tree." Said Raphael.

I was speechless. If I obeyed this request I would lose my immortality. I would be turned into a normal mortal and be cursed to walk amongst the mortals as a normal human being. Or my vessel would perish almost instantly.

"Someone will be visiting you." Said Raphael now, changing his tone to a much more pleasant tone.

"This someone will come without warning. This someone will help you on your journey to the Garden. But in the end its you that must partake of the fruit." He said now looking towards the ground of the basement.

I pondered the request before replying.

"Let's say I don't do this. Then what happens to me?" I asked.

Tears begin to form in the corner of Raphel's blue ocean eyes.

"What happens to me?" I asked again.

"Then you'll shift and die." Said Raphael.

It was silent. No more words were spoken between me and my brother.

He backed away slowly into the shadows of the basement. The last thing I saw was his hands coming together, making a hand-clap. The noise ringed my ears. He was gone. As for the church members above I heard them shuffling about, above me. They were back to normal. Everything was back to normal, including Pastor John. His memory had been wiped of the entire encounter with both of us. I could hear him mumbling from above.

"You must rebuke Satan. In the Lord's name. You must rebuke him so he doesn't get his foot in the door!" Said Pastor John's voice that traveled down into the basement where I was.

I pulled out a chair from the table in the basement and sat down.

I put my hands against my face, shielding my eyes.

I started to weep.

Morningstar Chapter 10

I wept. The palms of my hands shielded my eyes. I didn't know what to do. If I obeyed, I would be turned into a mortal. If I disobeyed I would shift and die. Either way, I was screwed. I knew what partaking of the fruit would do. Raphael was just sent as a messenger from Father. These were his commands. But let me take you back for a moment. Let me take you back to the beginning, back to, *The Garden*.

IN THE BEGINNING, THERE was *The Garden*. There were many trees within the garden, each one of them distinguishable from the other. Each one of them blossoming with food of different varieties. All throughout *The Garden* was harmony. With harmony brought blessings to the humans that were bound to be within *The Garden*, upon God's commands. The humans were blessed with the knowledge of what trees they could eat from. They were also told what trees not to eat. For miles upon miles all the eye could see in *The Garden* was trees of fruit. One stuck out above all the rest on a hill. *The Forbidden Tree*. It is an ancient and divine tree within The Garden. The tree reached the highest peaks of Heaven. Where Father oversaw everything. It was here he sat upon his throne in the highest part of Heaven, watching over Adam and Eve within The Garden.

Adam and Eve were perfect in all their ways. Except one thing. They were curious. After all it was Dad that made them that way. It wasn't my fault I was free to roam in The Garden. That's when I saw her. Eve. She was admiring *The Forbidden Tree*.

"CURIOUS ARE WE?" I asked Eve.

"Father said we can't eat from this tree, but its fruit looks so good." Said Eve while studying the wind blowing among the leaves of *The Forbidden Tree*.

"Father says many things, Eve," I said while glancing at the tree myself.

"Why would he grant you the right to eat from all these trees but this one in particular?" I asked her.

"I don't know." She answered while showing a saddened face.

"Why allow you and Adam to partake from every tree here but this one. Its fruit looks the most delicious of all the fruits." I said while studying the fruit.

"I'm not sure." Was her reply.

"Haven't you always wondered why you are here? Why are you in The Garden? Why are you and Adam alive and breathing?" I asked.

"Yes, but Father told us all of this is ours but this one tree, I just want to know what it tastes like." She said curiously.

"Then why don't you take one?" I asked.

Her face was expressionless at first then her eyes became big and round.

"Take one?" She said while looking at me.

"Yes, just one for you and Adam to share. It will be our little secret," I said, smiling in her direction.

"I couldn't do that, could I?" She asked innocently.

The choice was hers, not mine. I couldn't make her do anything. All I knew was that Father had told me to come down to The Garden to check in on Eve and see what she was doing. I was just following orders.

"You can do anything you want Eve. The choice is simply up to you." I said, shrugging my shoulders.

We both paused and studied the tree for a moment. Counting every leaf, every branch. The sunlight glistened from behind the tree getting in our eyes ever so slightly to where she and I both had to shield our eyes from being blinded. The wind blew ever so slightly through the trees, bobbing the fruit that hung from the branches.

"The choice is up to me." She said looking in my direction while taking steps up to the tree. She was within arm's length of the nearest branch.

"The choice is up to you," I said.

That was all it took. She picked fruit from *The Forbidden Tree* and instantly devoured a big chunk of the juicy brightly colored fruit within her hand. Her eyes rolled back into her head. She dropped the fruit, jaw wide open looking back at me. Then she snapped out of it. Whatever had happened when she had eaten from the tree made her more knowledgeable of her surroundings and who and what she was. More importantly, it made her more self-aware. She was frightened by the knowledge she had just received from eating from the tree. So she ran. She ran away from me, she ran away from Father, in search of Adam to tell him of what she had done.

I stood there idly by the tree as I wondered if I should have stopped her in some way or some form. But, my orders were clear. Check on Eve in *The Garden* and report back to me. That was the last thing I was told. Although in my heart I wondered if I had done something I shouldn't have. About that time Father summoned me.

"Yes, Father," I said out loud in all directions.

"What do you mean what have I done?" I asked.

He was communicating with me in my head. This was one of many ways we spoke with each other.

"All I said was the choice was simply up to her." I thought with confusion.

The next few things were that of a blur. I thought of ways I could make things better for Adam and Eve. Things that Father hadn't thought of. Things that I thought would be better for everything and everyone. Then I was cast out. I fell from grace as I had told you earlier in my story. All because I questioned why I was being questioned. All because I didn't stop Eve. All because I was following orders in the first place to go check on Eve in the Garden.

So there I was still in the church basement. Wondering why and what I was going to do. All I knew was one thing was for certain. If I had to do this, I was going to do it on my terms. I was done crying. I was done feeling sorry for myself. I was done playing by the rules. I needed to find Gabriel.

MorningStar Chapter 11

I quickly got to my feet. I shrugged my shoulders because my wings were feeling restless, under the suit jacket I was wearing. I realized I would have to try my luck at reaching out to Gabriel again. It was just a matter of how I had to figure it out. Remember me mentioning that I couldn't communicate with my brothers or Father, with my thoughts? At the very least I knew the mortal prayer to Gabriel just as I knew the prayer to Michael. At least this time hopefully I wouldn't get my ass kicked. Gabriel had a lot more patience, with me than Michael did.

I needed to get out of the church, out of the basement. I needed to go find somewhere quiet that would bring forth Gabriel to me.

Out the backdoor that was down in the basement, I went. Out and around back onto the gravel parking lot of the church where the Charger was parked. I jumped over the driver's side door and into the driver's seat. I grabbed the steering wheel with both hands gripping the leather ever so slightly. I reached into my right black suit pocket where I had put the keys earlier. I could hear the metal keys clanking about in my pocket. I started the car. The engine roared. I gave it some acceleration while still having it in park.

I turned the radio up. The DJ was talking.

"105.7 The Rock, brings you this next song from a listener request from Nashville.

"Highway to Hell by AC/DC." Said the DJ in a deep voice.

The beginning lyrics and guitar rift started blaring through the speakers of the Charger. I adjusted the center mirror and admired my facial features for a moment. My chiseled jawline and bone structure in my cheeks never had quite looked so good. These modern-day caffeine drinks did a serious number to Mortals, but man did it make us angels look and feel good. I put the car in reverse, turning the steering wheel as I backed up. I knew where to go. I needed to go back to the cornfield on the outskirts of town. The place where Michael and I had fought. It was there I could attempt to summon Gabriel. The church was still in session. The engine was blaring. "Highway to Hell " lyrics and guitar riffs were playing through the radio. I peeled out. I mean I peeled out of the gravel parking lot, kicking up rocks as I went. I knew flying would be faster. But I just had to get out of sight before I could take off. It wouldn't be good to be caught. Not today. My head was already spinning with the choice I had to make.

Take and eat from the Tree, or perish by shifting. I had already experienced the beginning stages of shifting earlier. I wasn't quite sure I wanted to experience that again.

"From dust, we came, and dust we shall return," I said out loud.

So I drove. I drove back onto the highway, back towards the Casey's General Store, where Zoey the gas station attendant graciously let me borrow her boyfriend's Charger. What? You didn't think I was that heartless, did you? Of course, I was going to return it. After all, I said I was only going to borrow it.

The wind blew through my thick blondish hair. It had a hint of brown in it. I could see it blowing on account of the rearview mirror. I was headed east on the highway back to Casey's.

"Speak of the devil and he shall appear," I muttered as I passed by a highway patrolman.

I knew he was clocking vehicles. I didn't care enough at the moment to slow down.

"Such stupidity, mortal laws of speed limits." I thought.

I looked down at the speedometer. I was pushing nearly one hundred miles an hour in a speed zone of eighty miles per hour.

"Dammit. I should have been faster." I thought out loud chuckling.

About that time the siren lights lit up from behind me. The highway patrolman was gaining on me. I pulled over to the right side of the road and came to a complete stop. I could tell he was fuming mad by the way he slammed his patrol car door. I watched him out of the driver's side mirror, start his walk up to my borrowed vehicle. His hands were placed carefully on his gun ever so slightly. I wasn't worried about his gun. Guns were the least of a fallen angel's concern. Especially after I had been restored to my full power. After eight energy drinks and a hot coffee, I was. The top was down on the Charger, the Tennessee summer heat felt good beating down on me.

The officer was furious as he approached my driver's side door.

"License and registration." Said the officer while sighing, and looking me up and down.

"Of course officer," I said as I pretended to reach for my non-existent wallet.

"Do you have any idea how fast you were going?" He asked.

"Honestly since we are telling the truth here, I knew I was going at least one hundred miles an hour," I said smirking.

Cars were whizzing by us on the busy highway. I did my best to pull to the curb, I had been driving since the launch of the Model T, after all. Driving wasn't something new to me.

"That's right. You were going twenty miles over the speed limit. Now I need your license and registration, Mr–?" He said, asking for a last name.

"MorningStar. Mr. Lucifer MorningStar is the name" I said smiling even more.

"Do you think this is funny?" He asked in a pissed-off tone.

His patience was running thin.

"Of course, I find it funny, Mr–?" I asked.

His blank stare told it all. I was pressing his buttons.

"Patterson. Paul Patterson." He replied fuming.

"Well PP," I said, chuckling.

"This is your last warning. License and registration." He said hand now on his pepper spray vile and his other hand on his radio that slung across his chest.

"Oh, Paul. There's no reason to do that," I said while glaring into his eyes.

He instantly was under my control.

"There's no reason for me to do that." Said Officer Patterson in a monotone voice.

He was at a standstill.

"You're going to let me go," I said while still keeping eye contact with him.

I moved my head to the left, he moved his to the left. I moved my head to the right and he followed to the right.

"I'm a freaking snake charmer of mortals!" I shouted while lifting my hands in the air with joy.

"You're a freaking snake charmer of mortals." Said Officer Patterson, still under my control.

I laughed with delight. I was having way too much fun.

"You're going to let me go now," I said while glaring deep into his eyes.

"I'm going to let you go now." Said Officer Patterson.

"Sounds good to me, Officer PP. Thanks for letting me go, it won't happen again." I said while adjusting my sunglasses back onto my face.

I turned the radio on, cranking it up to max volume, and peeled out, away from Officer PP, back onto the highway, and further towards the Casey's General Store.

MorningStar Chapter 12

It wasn't long before I was parked outside Casey's General Store. I killed the engine and lifted myself out of the driver's seat and over the side of the Charger. What? You didn't think I'd honestly return it? Shame on you, for doubting me. I walked inside the store and dropped the keys at the counter.

Zoey was clueless. She had let me borrow it after I had asked her for the keys. Yes, of course, I had to persuade her a bit, but that was in the past. The car was safe and sound and I was on my way back out of the store. I rounded the back of the store, looking at my surroundings. Trash was littered everywhere and the smell was that of mildew and sewage. Humans were a lost cause for the most part. They didn't care about their precious environment. By my calculations alone I estimated they'd be wiped from the planet within the next one hundred years if they didn't start taking care of the planet better.

I took my jacket off and threw it to the ground. I started to unbutton my shirt, button by button. I started to wiggle my shoulders and my wings were restless. I threw the shirt to the ground watching it land near the black jacket that I was wearing. My wings were exposed. Out they came in full length. My black wings raised above my head. I ruffled up my feathers to take flight. I smiled to my left and right looking at my wing span. No mortals were in sight. I did a slight jump into the air before bringing my wings down toward the ground. I was hovering. Maybe six or seven feet off of the ground. Then just like that, I was gone. Off I went in search of my brother Gabriel.

I had been flying for quite a while. High above the clouds. The range of eyesight for an angel was like that of a hawk. We could see the ground from miles above. I knew I was nearing the cornfield again. I saw the irrigator that Michael had thrown me into. It was bent up slightly, where I had impacted it. I touched down in the cornfield gracefully. Careful was key, otherwise, I'd leave a crop circle, or even worse catch the ground on fire. If I impacted the ground just right as I learned centuries ago I could even leave a crater impact. Just like the one I had left in Arizona all those years ago. The scientists had blamed it on a "Meteor" but in all honesty, it was me, from whenever I had been cast out.

I rested my wings and pulled them in close to my shoulders.

"Now how do I get you here brother?" I said out loud.

I needed a way to contact Gabriel. Then it occurred to me. I could simply just say the prayer to him. I drew a circle in the cornfield around me and looked at my work. I traced the circle carefully with my right wing all around me. Plenty big enough for two people to enter the circle.

"Bless this circle and all ye who enter it." I prayed.

What? Yes, I still had tricks up my sleeves. What I was doing was creating a binding circle. The caster could enter and leave the circle whenever they wished, but the bound could not. Just a simple precaution in case Gabriel was going to act like Michael. I wasn't fixing to get my ass royally handed to me, by my younger brother. Not today. The wind was blowing from the west, I had about three or four hours of sunlight left. Everything was in order.

I took a breath and started the prayer. I raised my hands and wings towards the sky.

"O blessed Archangel Gabriel, I beseech thee, May your light fill me with the Holy Spirit. May you come forth and protect me against my enemies both spiritually and physically."

I paused. It was working. All around me the wind started to shift and started blowing in all directions. Pieces of corn were flying up off the stalks. Then from out of the sky, I saw. It was Gabriel. What started as a small spec in the sky was growing larger and larger. He was coming down with such a fury. Then as violent as he was coming down, he gently flapped his wings twice before touching down in the circle. He kneeled, head down, wings covering his head and body, before spreading them out and extending them.

"Lucifer. I should have known." He said with annoyance.

"Wow, I'm quite surprised that it even worked," I said joyfully.

He stood up. He was much smaller than my other two brothers. But he was a force to be reckoned with. For he was the protector of Father's people. The messenger of God, as he was called. In some languages, his name was translated to mean "The strength of God."

"I don't need this right now," He said as he turned his back towards me.

He started to walk towards the outer edges of the binding circle I had drawn in the dirt. Then it hit him. Like a force field. He couldn't leave the binding circle. He was bound to it.

"Curse you, brother!" He said angrily.

"Brother, I need you to listen to me. I wouldn't have called you if it wasn't important." I said, trying to reason with him.

He turned back around facing me with his fists clenched.

"Make it fast." He said unclenching his fists.

"I'm so glad to see that you are okay. That means Michael got to you in time." I said while taking a step towards him.

He started to nod.

"Yes, he found me. He told me of what happened between you two before I started to ascend." He said, staring at the ground for a moment before making eye contact with me again.

"That's all I wanted. Was for you to be okay." I said as I smirked.

I breathed air out of my lungs.

"What's your other question?" Asked Gabriel.

" I need to know why you sacrificed yourself off the cliff instead of fighting me," I said.

The air was silent. For several seconds not a word was spoken nor a sound could be heard. Then he responded.

"Because Lucifer, you're my brother. More importantly, your story isn't finished yet. You still have unfinished matters th—-." He said while pausing.

"The rest doesn't matter," He said, fluffing up his wings.

"The rest doesn't matter?" I asked.

His patience was running thin.

"Lucifer. You must return to Kansas." He said forcefully.

"Kansas?" I asked.

"Why Kansas?" I wondered.

"Because." Said Gabriel while snapping.

"I don't understand why the hell I would go back to Kansas," I said.

Gabriel stared at the ground for several seconds then responded.

"Because you have a daughter," Gabriel said.

"A what?" I asked.

"That's all I'm bound to tell you, Lucifer. Now let me go."

My heart sank into my chest.

"A daughter?" I said out loud while rubbing my eyes as tears were beginning to form in my eyes.

I had never been a father before, nor had any children that I could call my own.

"But I thought angels, can't, you know," I said to Gabriel.

"Can't create life? They're not supposed to do other things as well, but here we are, aren't we." He said, smirking.

"Oh like you've never," I said, snapping at him.

"That's not the point Lucifer. The point is besides you eating from the tree in The Garden you must also return to Kansas." He said taking a step towards me.

We were now only a few feet apart. The sun was beginning to set.

"Now what exactly am I supposed to do in Kansas, once I get there?" I asked Gabriel.

Only one word was spoken as he laid his hand over my chest.

"Love." He said.

"Just simply, love." He said, patting me on the chest.

I was speechless. No words were being said.

"Why am I just now learning that I have a daughter?" I asked.

Gabriel shook his head.

"Now you want to be a father? Now you care? After planting your seed in a mortal!" He shouted.

He had me on that one.

"Wait. Rachel? Rachel Fairborn?" I asked.

Gabriel nodded his head, in an up-and-down motion.

"So Rachel Fairborn had the daughter of Lucifer MorningStar," I said while scratching my chin and looking at the ground.

I was in shock. The possibility of a fallen angel having a kid with an angel was unheard of.

I honestly thought I couldn't create life. I thought I was sterile.

"Now let me go out of this binding circle, brother." Said Gabriel.

I walked towards the outer edges of the circle, destroying the circle by kicking around the loose dirt where I had originally drawn the circle. The circle was now disrupted. Gabriel walked out of the circle and away from me. I still had questions but he was done with all of this.

"Just one more question, before you go," I said while holding my finger up in the air in his direction.

He jumped and started to hover. His wings folded downwards keeping him off of the ground by about a few feet. He looked in my direction, his eyes were the color of a lush green meadow.

"What's her name, my daughter?" I asked, trying to speak over his wings flapping.

Gabriel was now twenty or so feet into the air. Then he responded.

"Her name is Grace." He said as he left, rising above the clouds.

I couldn't make out where Gabriel had gone. I didn't care. I was just glad he was Okay.

"Grace is it," I said to myself.

With the sun setting almost completely, I jumped and started to hover in the cornfield. My wings had never felt better.

"Looks like your old man is fixing to pay you a visit," I said smiling before taking off above the clouds.

MorningStar Chapter 13

The moonlight lit my way high above the clouds. It had to be nearly midnight by now. I had been flying for several hours. The night was beyond cold. I looked down and around to pick up where I was at. I flapped my wings to rise even higher. Looks like Missouri. I knew my general direction, but to be honest I didn't feel like flying all night to get to Kansas from Tennessee. It didn't matter though. None of that mattered. I was committed. I had a daughter.

"How old was she?" I wondered.

"Was she one of those annoying pre-teens, with a cell phone and an attitude?" I asked myself.

I tried to remember the last time I had well you know, with Rachel.

I quickly shook myself out of asking any more questions.

"Rachel." I thought.

"Rachel Fairborn," I said out loud while flapping my wings again.

Not only was she the mother of my child, but she was also a total babe. Her blonde hair touched down to her waist, and was almost always straight or curly, depending on what she did with her hair that day. Honestly, I didn't fall for mortals, it gets too complicated, but her? I'd fall for her thousand times over. Her eyes were the color of sapphire. They were like calm spring rain. Not too much and not too little. Her beauty was unbecoming. The story of how we met was one of a kind. Wrong place, right time. Here, we have plenty of time, before we get to Kansas, I'll just tell you the story.

"WELCOME TO BEANS AND Brew." Said the woman behind the counter at the coffee house.

I was suffering from a major head injury. I had fallen after drinking a little too much all night. Honey Whiskey is delicious. What? You're judging me? Seriously after everything we've been through up to this point. Anyways I digress. I had a major head injury after falling off the roof of my condo. I thought I had my wings ready, but in my drunken mindset, they were not. Plus, the hangover. The awful aching in the temple on the side of my head. I needed caffeine. Lots of it. Luckily for me, this coffee shop would give me unlimited amounts of espresso shots in my coffee. The new girl behind the counter welcomed me again.

"Hi there. Welcome to Beans and Brew." She said to me again.

The smell of roasted coffee beans filled my nostrils. The ambient lo-fi music kept a slow and steady beat. The volume wasn't too high, but to me, it was obnoxiously loud. Angels also had keen hearing abilities. We could hear from miles around us if we tuned in and narrowed the location of noise with our hearing ability. I rubbed the temple of my head, with annoyance, everything was so loud. I needed caffeine immediately. There was nobody in the coffee shop but me and the new girl behind the counter.

"Rough night? I got just the trick for that." She said as she tapped the counter and walked away briefly.

She started to make espresso.

"Mmm, my favorite," I said to her.

"Good, I'm making it special just for you Mr-?"

I was lost in a daze, her backside was turned to me as she was making the drink for me. I started to think with other things other than my head. She turned around to see if I was going to answer, and her smile caught my attention.

"MorningStar," I said while clearing my throat.

"Just like the Bible?" She said excitedly.

"Precisely like the Bible," I said now grinning at her while I studied her from top to bottom.

I leaned against the counter. She was still making the drink.

"Okay, I'll bite," I said while knocking my right and left fists against the counter ever so slightly.

She had a puzzled look for a second before turning back around and continuing to make the drink.

"What's your name?" I asked intriguingly.

She smiled, she was intrigued as well.

"Rachel. Rachel Fairborn." She said while putting a top on the drink.

"Like the Bible?" I said.

"Precisely like the Bible," said Rachel while handing the drink over to me on the counter.

"Is that for me?" I asked.

She was wearing a multitude of different bracelets along her wrist. Some were different shades of black. Some of them were shades of purple and green. I studied them briefly for a moment. Her hair was golden, it passed down her backside almost to her waist.

"Yup all yours, what's your first name?" She asked.

I reached for the drink, downing it within seconds. I took a breath to clear the hot espresso I had just drunk in seconds from my throat. The warm coffee burned the back of my throat, but I didn't care. She had added some secret ingredient that I couldn't quite put my finger on.

"Lucifer," I responded.

She was beyond intrigued, by both my name and my skills with downing the coffee in seconds. She leaned forward on the counter.

"Well, Lucifer MorningStar. What are you doing later this evening?" She asked while giving me that beautiful smile.

I was sold. I couldn't shake her. The only thing that was on my mind was her.

"Looks like my evening just cleared up. What do you have in mind?" I asked Rachel.

She grabbed my wrist and turned over the palm of my right hand. She pulled out a pin and started to write what appeared to be her number on my palm, in black ink.

"This is my address. You can come over after seven-thirty." She said with confidence.

I had never met a mortal with such confidence and that knew exactly what they wanted. I knew what I wanted, and I wasn't going to stop until I got what was mine.

"I'm looking forward to it," I said.

"Your total will be $6.25," She said.

I was bewildered. I thought she had hooked me up with the drink.

"Wait really?" I asked.

She chuckled while letting go of my wrist and palm.

"No. I'm just messing with you." She said while still chuckling.

Her laugh was otherworldly. It was unique in all its ways.

"Funny are we?" I asked.

She stood up with her hands on her hips. Her hair had covered half of her right eye. She blew it out of her face with her mouth.

"You have no idea." She said to me.

"Well thank you for the free coffee. Although I must ask what was that sweet flavor you added to the drink, I couldn't quite put my finger on it?" I asked her.

Her eyes connected with mine. I was lost in them.

"It's honey," She responded.

"How sweet," I said while containing the burning that was happening inside of me.

I wanted her. I stared at her, making eye contact.

"I'll tell you what I'm off at six. How about you come over at six-thirty instead of seven-thirty?" She said, clearing her throat.

She was clearly thinking with other things other than her head.

"I'll see you then Rachel Fairborn," I said before adjusting the jacket I was wearing and exiting the coffee shop.

My headache was gone now. As for my head injury, it had healed almost completely. My stomach gurgled. I was hungry. Luckily for me I had dinner plans lined out, and I couldn't wait because I was famished.

WHAT? YOU DIDN'T THINK I'd dive further into detail than that did you? How naughty. I was nearing the outskirts of the town of Haven, Kansas. The sweet aroma of wheat filled my nostrils. I had been flying all night to make it to this point. I had to touch down somewhere that I couldn't be caught. Remember it was one of the rules I followed. If a mortal was to catch me, the result would be catastrophic. Not only would I turn instantly to dust, but the mortal(s) that saw me in my angelic form would also more than likely die instantly as well. I had to get as close to the coffee shop as possible. The sun was nearing its rise in the east. Birds had started to chirp and come alive for the morning. I touched down behind a farmhouse. Nobody was awake. There were no nearby lights so I remained in the shadows behind an old barn as I collected myself. My hands were on my knees.

"Man I'm out of shape," I said to myself.

I hadn't flown that long in a while. The sun was continuing its rise. A nearby oil well was making its ticking noise on the property. *Tick tick tick tick tick.* It was a mechanized noise that never faltered nor skipped a beat. I needed a shirt. Anything at this point would be fine for me. I could retract my wings for the most part. It was an annoying process, but I couldn't risk showing them off to anybody in the community. A clothesline full of hanging clothes just happened to be within reach around the front of the barn. If I could just get a shirt, I'd be on my way. I walked in front of the barn and that's when I saw it on a zipline connected to the barn, to a nearby oak tree. A Doberman. A dog of this caliber didn't need to be awoken from its slumber. I carefully walked over to the clothesline and started shuffling through the clothes. A white buttoned-up long-sleeve shirt that just so happened to appear in my size.

"Perfect," I thought to myself.

I unclipped the shirt from the clothesline and put on the shirt carefully closing my wings. I shook back and forth to shuffle the bottom part of my wings down into my pants. I buttoned each button up one by one and let out a sigh of relief. That's when I heard it.

Growling from behind me. The doberman had awoken.

MorningStar Chapter 14

"Nice doggy," I said.

The Doberman wasn't having it. In fact, the growls and the showing of its teeth told me I should be very careful backing away. Except I was pinned to walk only one way. If I went forward I'd be heading back behind the barn. If I went backward like the dog wanted me to, I'd run straight into the farmhouse porch. I put my hands up in the air to try and show the dog I meant no harm. I slowly shifted in a half circle with my back now towards the farmhouse.

"Easy there boy," I said to the dog.

The dog started to bark ferociously. So much so that I was worried he'd wake up the homeowners. He had me backed up almost to the porch. I had to do something.

"Come on boy, all I wanted was a shirt, that's all I took," I said to the now terrifying Doberman.

His teeth were showing. His ears were pointed straight up, and his face was nothing but pure aggression. He repeatedly opened and shut his jaws, barking and growling louder and louder. But, what am I even doing in this situation? I've handled dogs before. This one would be no different. He went to lunge at me with his mouth wide open. That's when I did it. I snapped my fingers and the dog froze instantly. He gently touched the ground on all fours with his mouth wide open still frozen.

"Charlie, what's wrong!" Shouted a distant voice from the farmhouse.

It was the farmer standing on his porch.

"Hey! You there, stop right there or I'll blow your head clean off!" Said the farmer.

I heard the cocking of a shotgun from the porch, I was just within range of the shotgun.

"Oh shit," I said as I started to make a run for it, out of the backyard into the wheat field by the barn.

The farmer fired a shot and missed.

"Yeah, you better run you, rat bastard!" Said the farmer before firing another shot in my direction.

At this point, I had done a zig-zag pattern with the way I was running toward the wheat field.

"Get 'em, Charlie." Said the farmer in the distance behind me.

Charlie was taking a little nap though. I had forgotten to unfreeze him. Luckily for me, I was out of range of the shotgun and had made my way into the semi-tall wheat field. I raised my hands semi-level to my chest and clapped them together, letting out a thunderous boom. Just like Rapheal had done in the basement of the church, to unfreeze everybody in the church.

"Charlie my boy you're okay," I heard the farmer say in the far distance.

His focus was on his dog, and I was on the run in the middle of the wheat field. At least I had a shirt. I needed to find my way into town. The way I touched down back at the farmhouse, if I just kept heading east, I was sure to find the town eventually. The sun was beginning to rise over the horizon. The colder weather was starting to dissipate. The warm morning sun was taking charge in the sky for the day. I had to be over a mile or two away from the farm. Still miles of wheat to the left and right side of me. I could see a clearing in the road up ahead. A few cars whizzed by. From what I could see it was a harmless road leading into town.

"Maybe I could get a ride," I thought.

What? You honestly think I'm going to continue to walk, after I flew all night, and almost got killed by that farmer and his scary dog?

I could see my breath come out of my mouth. It was colder here in Kansas than it was in Tennessee. Cars continued to whiz by. It wasn't extremely busy, it was your typical county road. I recalled where I was, as I came out of the wheatfield. I knew further down the county road behind me, was the little country church for the town of Haven. I looked for any traffic coming my way and other than that of a little farmtruck, there was nothing.

It was a little elderly man driving. He watched me as I came out of the wheat field. He had the most confused look on his face as he passed me by. I didn't think I'd get a ride from him anyways. Me and elderly people often didn't mix. I remember one time I was chased out of Haven with holy water and pitchforks. True story. It gives me the creeps. But let's focus on this story.

Further into town was the coffee house Rachel, worked at all those years ago. I thought I'd see if she was at work before proceeding to her place. I wasn't even sure if she still lived at the same address to be honest.

So there I was walking down the county road toward town. I was coming up on a bridge, and a mileage sign. The mileage sign read:

"Haven- Three Miles".

I was nearly there. Regardless if it seemed dead around here, there was always a typical farmer or rancher. The only reason I bring this up is that I couldn't get caught changing into my angelic form. So walking was the only choice here unless I got a ride. See angels had three forms. One is the mortal form. This form was what we used to walk amongst the masses, hidden among everybody. We appeared completely normal. The second is the angelic form. This is your typical angel with wings, flying around. This was one of the condemned forms. If you were deemed turning into this form in front of mortals then the consequences would be dire. Stripped of powers, shifting phase, and then ultimately turning into dust.

Third is True form. I hadn't been able to appear in my true form since I had been cast out of Heaven. This is the biblical sense of what angels appeared as in the bible. Some people imagine angels to look like little children with halos and tiny wings. Floating around in the heavens playing their little harps. This is wrong. True form is our spirit form. Since we are spirit beings this makes us immortal. **Revelation 4:8** mentions four living creatures before God's throne that had six wings and were covered with eyes all around, even under their wings. For ages, man has questioned exactly what angels look like, which is why it's so important to follow the golden rule. Don't expose yourself to mortals unless instructed to. If you're instructed to, usually you come to mortals in mortal form.

I used to be so beautiful in my True form. I was a Cherubim, at least I used to be. In **Ezekiel 1:10** Ezekiel's vision of God Cherubims is described as having four wings. Two for covering their feet, and two for flight and have four faces: a Human, a lion, an ox, and an eagle. Our names meant "fulfillment of wisdom". Now I was cursed to walk in my angelic form or my mortal form. I could never be fully restored to walking in my true form.

I wasn't far from town now, about a mile out. A red old tractor was out in the field to the left of me, plowing the field. An old farm truck passed by me slowly. Another old man. I definitely wasn't going to get a ride at this rate. So there I was walking down the road one foot in front of the other. The town was coming into view. A few cars passed me by slowly, getting into the other lane as they came across me. No one stopped. I didn't expect them to stop. Most mortals didn't care for hitchhikers. Another ten minutes or so and I'd be in the main part of town where the coffee house, "Beans and Brew" was.

In front of me, on the right-hand side coming up was the community baseball field. No one of course was there. On the left was an empty field with planted seed. Probably barley. Haven was a quiet farming community. Not too much happened here, which was perfect for me to lay low back in the day. I had originally been in Haven, Kansas because I had been on a drinking binge. Until that one day, I fell off the roof of a random building late one night and hit my head. You would think that it wouldn't hurt me, on the premise that only other angels could hurt each other. Normally physical damage wouldn't be a factor, but in this case, because I was drinking it did.

Drinking in angels caused the immortal factor to be a little different. If an angel drank enough, they'd be vulnerable to physical damage. So when I say I hurt myself when I hit my head, after falling off the building, I did. That's where the coffee from Beans and Brew came into play. On occasion, I visited this brick-and-mortar coffee house built into the main street building. Their espresso shots mixed in with my coffee drinks were wake-up juice for me. That's when I met her as I told you earlier, Rachel. It had been years since I had talked to her. I had no recollection of mortal time, but if I was to take a stab at it, I think it had been eight or nine years. Which in theory meant Grace was at least nine or fixing to be ten. That was the last time you know, we...

Anyways I digress, I had to find Rachel, even if she didn't want to see me. We had a falling out. The last I had talked to her she was throwing stuff at my head in her kitchen because I had gone out all night to drink.I wasn't a hitter. I'd never hit her. But I was a mess whenever I drank too much. She had told me to get out of her house, which is exactly what I did, and I never returned back to Haven. Now here we are nine years later, and I am back.

MorningStar Chapter 15

I was nearing the coffee house. There wasn't much on the main street where the Beans and Brew coffee house was. A local grocery store on the left. A family dollar on the right. Traffic came and went. The sun was nearing the highest point in the sky, which meant it was nearly noon or right after noon. I could smell the aroma of coffee beans coming from out of the shop. This was my chance to make amends with Rachel. If I could just apologize to her again then maybe she would forgive me. I tried to apologize nine years ago, but I was drunk. So drunk that I was stumbling over myself and things were fading in and out. Yes, it was one of my poisons. But after that fight that night, I barely ever touched the stuff anymore. On occasion, I'd have a drink, but the mood had to strike me. Usually if I was pissed off, I drank. It calmed my nerves. Most of the time I was always pissed. Always full of rage. But that's because I hated Father, for what he did. To be honest most of you knew only half of the story.

The "devil" as you call him thought he was better than God, and led a mutiny, against him in Heaven to try and overthrow him. The honest truth? I knew I was better than him. I also understood he had created me, and this was his game with his rules I was playing by. If everything was as it had been, all I wanted was to change a few things. If he gave us angels free will as he did mortals then he had always known that one day I would try to overthrow him. He already knew when he created me, that one day he'd cast me out of the heavens. It's not that I didn't want to worship Father anymore, it's simply the fact that

I wanted to become a God just like Father, so I could help him in his services because I knew how to make the world and the heavens just a little better in my image. It's crazy to think about but put yourself in my shoes. I loved him with all my being and to be cast out like that, was so wrong. I even meant it when I asked for forgiveness but it was too late. We were past that. Here I was thousands of years later fixing to meet a mortal I had fallen for almost a decade ago.

I opened the door to the Beans and Brew coffee house, and the little bell on the doorbell rang. It was supposedly used to ward off evil spirits. It didn't work. I adjusted my collar and ran my hand through my thick black hair adjusting myself for presentation purposes.

"Hi, welcome to Beans and Brew!" Said a barista behind the counter.

"Hello there," I said.

"What can I get for you?" Said the barista cheerfully.

"I'm looking for someone, maybe you can help," I said.

I leaned on the counter and the memories came flooding back in. It was as if I had never left. All those times ordering my triple shot of espresso came back to me.

"Who are you looking for?" Asked the barista.

She was practically a teenager. A young thing, no older than seventeen if I had to guess. By the looks of it, she hadn't been working there very long.

"I'm looking for Rachel Fairborn. I'm an old friend of hers and I just wanted to stop by and say hello to her." I said while peering my eyes toward the back of the coffee house.

She was nowhere in sight.

"Oh, you must not know." Muttered the barista.

"Must not know what?" I said.

She paused briefly. She wasn't responding to my question.

I snapped my finger in her direction. This quickly got her attention.

"Must not know what?" I said louder and clearer.

"Rachel took some time off about a month ago. She was sick. Real sick. Turns out she has ovarian cancer and now she's on hospice care at her house. " She said with a sad face.

My heart sank into my chest. The only thing that could be heard as she continued to explain the situation to me, was white noise. Her voice was fading in and out.

"The doctors aren't sure exactly how long she has." She said.

I was in disbelief. I couldn't comprehend the words I was being told.

She kept talking but I wasn't picking up on anything she was saying. If only I had been here. If only I hadn't left. Maybe I could have done something to prevent this. Maybe I could still prevent it.

"And that's how we think she only–" She said before I cut her off.

"Where is Rachel?" I asked.

"Whoa, look I just can't be giving out her address like that, she's in no condi–" She said.

I slammed my hands down on the counter. The noise rattled throughout the quiet coffeehouse. After all it was just her and I. I wasn't having it. I needed to find Rachel. I made eye contact with the barista.

She was under my control.

"Where is Rachel!" I shouted while maintaining eye control with her.

She was in a trance. Her body language shifted to that of a stiff board. Her arms were perfectly in place not moving an inch.

"She's at home." She said.

"Where is home?" I demanded.

She was muttering the address.

"720 Willow Ave," She said.

That's all I needed. I snapped my finger and she came out of the trance.

"As I said, I can't tell you where she's at dude." She said now out of the trance.

"I understand," I said.

I got the address, I got what I needed.

I didn't have time to continue the conversation. I collected myself and exited the coffee shop and started heading toward 720 Willow Ave.

MorningStar Chapter 16

I wasn't far from the address. Rachel over the course of the last nine years or so had moved out of the apartment she had once lived at, and into a quiet nice neighborhood within the town of Haven.. I took a right down the street corner of Willow Avenue. Just a few more half blocks and I would be there. I wasn't walking by any means. I was speed walking. I had to get to her. I had to see her.

Just then out of the corner of my eye I saw wildflowers growing on the corner of the street. Lots of variations, all of them with their own distinct set of smells. Of course, I had to take this opportunity to pick some for Rachel. I started out by picking the shades of yellow and purple, followed by picking orange and shades of bright red. I had a handful now. A house was coming up on the right-hand side. On the left-hand side of the road was nothing but thick woods. Not a house in sight on the left. Just tree after tree.

"718 Willow Avenue." I said as I passed by the mailbox at the end of a driveway.

I was only one house away. It was the house that I was drawn to. The house I had been looking at from a distance. For some reason there was something drawing me towards the house. I couldn't shake it. I looked down at the flowers for a moment that I was still grasping in my hand ever so tightly. I moved a purple flower and put it next to a red flower. I mixed and matched this way until I was content with the arrangement. My wings were restless again already. I adjusted my shoulders and rolled them ever so slightly to stretch out my confined wings. Everything about this street spoke volume. The neighborhood was cleaned up and there appeared to only be three or four houses on the right side of the road before the road turned off into another road.

I could make out the lettering on the next mailbox. 720 Willow Avenue. As I got closer I made out that it was a black mailbox. On this mailbox was an adult's handprint and a child's handprint. Someone had dipped their hands in paint and put them on the metal black mailbox that read 720 Willow Avenue. If I was guessing it probably belonged to Rachel and Grace. A cluster of sunflowers rounded the mailbox.

"Rachel's favorite." I thought.

I looked at the flowers in my hand, and back at the sunflowers. I could easily exchange them for the sunflowers that lined her driveway. But I decided on leaving the sunflowers intact. I put my hand on the mailbox and measured my hand up to that of Rachel's. It was so much smaller than I remembered. Then I did the same with the child's handprint that I assumed was Grace's. It was beyond small. I started to walk up the driveway. There was a home nurse service van parked in the driveway next to a white Chevy Traverse. Pine trees lined the driveway on the right side. Pine needles were scattered everywhere. The smell of pine filled my nostrils. As I walked I could hear myself stepping on the small pine cones that had fallen from the tree onto the driveway. It wasn't the longest driveway, but just far enough from the street. A tin sign was attached to the house as I walked up the porch steps. It had a pair of angel wings wrapped in a four-leaf clover. The lettering on it said "Fairborn". I studied the symbol of the angel wings for a second which was wrapped around the four-leaf clover. This was probably on account of Rachel coming from Irish heritage. I remember the conversation with her while we were laying in bed one night. She went on to tell me that her great grandfather was from Ireland and migrated to America. The angel wings, well let's just say she might just like angels for some odd reason.

I was at the front door. A box of chalk was by the front door. The porch was a concrete slab that had chalk pictures drawn all over it. I looked down at them. A picture of an eye caught my attention. It was drawn out with pink chalk and yellow chalk. The artist must have been young because right below the eye were words, " I love you, mommy." In capital letters. A pink bicycle was on the left side of the end of the porch. It had pink tassels coming down off of the handlebars. On the back of the bike was a customized miniature license plate. It read "Too Fast". I took a deep breath in and exhaled as I knocked on the front door with flowers in my hand.

All was quiet. Then I heard the shuffling of little feet from inside. I saw the doorknob start to turn in front of me.

MorningStar Chapter 17

The door started to open up as I anxiously hoped that it would be Rachel.

A little girl answered the door, she couldn't be over ten years old. I had a knack for knowing mortals' age. She looked so precious. Could this little girl be my daughter? Her eyes were as blue as that of a cloudless blue sky. She looked up at me, connecting her eyes with mine and slowly blinked. No words were shared for a moment. There was something there. Something I couldn't quite put my finger on. This is what I had been feeling on my way up to the house. The same pull. I was staring at my daughter.

"Can I help you?" She asked in a saddened tone.

Something was bothering her, other than me being at the front door.

I wasn't sure what words to say to her. First impressions were, after all, everything.

"I'm Lucifer," I said.

It was the only words that came out of me.

She blew her brunette hair out of her face, further showing me her beautiful young blue eyes to me.

"Cool name. Like the Bible." She said.

"Precisely like the Bible," I said smiling.

It was deja vu all over again.

"And, what is your name if I may ask?" I said.

"My name is Grace." She said.

This was her. This was the daughter that Gabriel had told me about in the field. My heart was full of so much remorse and joy I could just jump with happiness. But I had to contain it. I couldn't just be like:

"Hi you may not know me but I was kicked out of Heaven thousands of years ago, and had sex with your mother and created you."

No. That wouldn't play over well. I had to ease myself into this situation.

"Well, Grace, I'm a friend of Rachel, your mother. I've come to see her if that's alright with you." I said.

Just then the home nurse came down the hallway, I could tell she was a home nurse on account of her uniform.

"Can I help you?" She asked.

She was now standing at the door pulling Grace away from the front door.

Grace was sad she was getting pulled away. She was already intrigued by our short little introduction.

I slowly realized I was beginning to rage. Only because she was pulling her away. I needed to calm my nerves. Otherwise, I was going to blow up. The last thing I needed was to blow up.

"This is Lucifer." Said Grace.

"He's here to see Mom." Said Grace looking up at the nurse.

The nurse looked down at Grace, before making eye contact with me.

"Look. Rachel isn't up for visitors right now, and quite frankly I don't know you, Mr. Lucifer." She said.

"MorningStar," I said, correcting her.

"Do what?" She said.

"You called me Mr. Lucifer. My name is Lucifer MorningStar. So if you were or are going to say my name in the form of mister, then I'd appreciate you calling me Mr. MorningStar.

Yes, I was a little upset and borderline territorial over Grace already. I couldn't help it. Something compelled me to act out in this manner. I was still on the outside of the door. The nurse had put herself between Grace and me. I looked deep into the nurse's eyes. She locked eyes with me. Time to work my magic.

"As I said, Rach–". She said before being in a trance.

It appeared as if Grace was none the wiser to what was taking place.

"You were saying Rachel will see me on account that I brought flowers, right?" I said.

The nurse's body language had changed completely. She was now moving out of the way and allowing me to come inside.

"Of course, you can, since you have flowers." She said while extending her hand to the inside of the house.

"Thank you," I said, taking a few steps into the entrance of the hallway of the house.

Grace was staring up at me, and then back at the flowers.

I could tell she wanted them for herself.

"Grace." She looked back up at me.

"I want you to have these flowers, but only if you promise to give some of them to Mom," I said while leaning down toward her and extending my hand with the flowers in it.

She took them. She studied the different colors while smiling at each different one.

"Okay. Okay, I can do that." She said before running off down the hallway and making a right.

"Well, what are you waiting for?" I heard Grace say.

"Do what?" I asked.

"You want to see Mom right?" Said Grace down the adjacent hallway.

Her voice carried down the hallway.

"Yes of course," I said now, making the nurse come out of the trance by snapping my fingers.

I walked past the nurse and made my way toward the start of the hallway.

Just then a voice from down the hallway responded.
"Grace, honey. Who is it?" Said the voice down the hallway.

MorningStar Chapter 18

The voice called again for Grace. It was very weak.

"Grace. Who? Who is it, sweetie?" said the voice from further down the hallway.

I was following Grace's lead. I saw her standing in the hallway with the flowers and then opening a door to what appeared to be a bedroom. The nurse walked casually behind me. I heard the voice again.

"Oh, flowers. Baby, you're so sweet. We can put them in water. Where did you get them from." Said the voice.

I was just a few steps from the bedroom.

"I didn't get them for you, Mommy. Your friend did." Said Grace.

"Oh, and who would that be?" I heard the voice reply.

I walked into the bedroom.

"It was Lucifer." Said Grace.

It was Rachel. She was in a hospital bed that was set up in the bedroom.

The look on her face could only be described as that of surprise. She wasn't expecting company, nor was she expecting to see me ever again.

She was hooked up to all kinds of machines and an IV drip was pumping drugs directly into the vein line on her right hand. She had an oxygen line connected to her nostrils. Incense was lit in the far corner of the room, the smoke trail changed and went upwards when I entered the room. Her face appeared drained. Her skin was sucked up, and her cheekbones were sunken in. Where her beautiful blonde hair once was, was nothing but a bald head. Not a hair in sight. She had drawn on her eyebrows where her hair once was. My heart sank deep into my chest. She looked away from me, as I was taking in the full effect of what was going on. What I was seeing. A single tear started to fall from her face while she was looking away. She didn't want me to see her in this condition. Grace was staring at both of us, trying to piece together what was happening before her. I walked over to Rachel's bedside. I gently wiped the tear from her face and rested my hand on her face. Her face was cold to the touch. I could feel the bone structure of her cheekbones and jawline.

She looked up at me with those beautiful blue eyes. Our eyes connected. One thing about Rachel and me is I had never performed any sort of tricks on her. I had never needed to. I was content with every emotion we had shared in the past. I wanted to feel when I was with her. We looked at each other for what felt like a lifetime. The tears had stopped coming down her face. With my hand still gently resting against hers, she took her left hand with all the strength she had and placed it against my hand while still staring up at me. She struggled to smile.

"Lu," She said. It was a pet name she had called me from time to time.

"Mommy he has a name just like the–." Said Grace before Rachel interrupted.

"Like the Bible." She said.

"Yep." Said Grace cheerfully.

Grace had the same shade of blue in her eyes as her mother. They were indistinguishable.

"Life has been moving so fast." She said to me.

It's as if those nine years had gone by in the blink of an eye. To a mortal, time seemed to move at a much slower pace. Nine years to an angel literally was nothing but a day or even a week. Our internal clocks were built differently. Would I have known that Rachel was sick or I had a daughter I wouldn't have ever left.

"I know babe. I know." I said rubbing her cheek line while smiling at her.

It's as if all was forgiven. The fight. The break-up. None of that mattered. Not now. Not at this moment. This moment was special. This moment was for her and me.

"How about that coffee?" I said.

"Do what?" she responded while slowly shifting in the bed.

"My head is killing me," I said jokingly while rolling my eyes.

"Oh is it? Well, I have just the thing for that." She said while blushing ever so lightly and extending her hands to me.

The IV line that was connected to Rachel lightly bumped against my shoulder.

The nurse had made her way into the room, Grace was still standing by with the flowers in hand, watching us interact.

We didn't care. We were completely in our element. I slightly leaned in for a kiss. Her lips connected with mine. When I tell you time stood still, it literally did. For at that moment it was just her lips connected with mine. It's as if we had never left each other. She grabbed my jawline and pulled me in with her all the strength that she had. It wasn't much. Her cold lips pressed hard against my lips as she drew in a breath, she was smiling. As was I.

"We need to check your vitals again Miss Fairborn." Said the nurse.

"Mommy." Said Grace.

The voices were fading in and out as they continued to try to talk while we kissed. I slowly backed my face away. Regardless of her condition, she was the most beautiful creation I had ever seen before. Rachel quickly regained her composure. As did I.

"Mom, why are you kissing Lucifer?" Asked Grace.

The nurse started to interject herself between us, which I was fine with. I took a few steps back as she started her work on Rachel. Rachel started to cough. A horrific cough that was full of phlegm. You could tell it was hurting her to cough. A few tears rolled down her face.

The nurse looked back at me while checking her oxygen levels. She slightly shook her head from left to right so as not to draw attention to herself from either Rachel or Grace. She was letting me know that the circumstances weren't good. The nurse took out a tissue and wiped Rachel's mouth with it. A few droplets of blood, soaked up the white tissue. I rubbed my head in disbelief. She wasn't doing well. Not in the slightest. Rachel continued to cough, this time clearing her lungs altogether of air and then gasping.

"Mommy." Said Grace, with worry.

Rachel made a fist with her right hand grasping at the bedding material she was laying on, still coughing. The nurse started to connect to her port which was connected to her lungs and started the draining process. Instantly a blackish fluid started to fill up the drain tube which was then transferred into a bladder bag. As the fluid drained out of her lungs I watched as her O2 stats started to dramatically improve. Then her grip let loose of the bedding material and she let out a gasp.

"There it is dear. We got it." Said the nurse while looking at Rachel.

"Slow steady breaths." Said the nurse.

"Mommy are you okay?" Said Grace.

Rachel cleared her throat and took in a deep but faint breath.

"Yes, sweetie. Mommy is fine. I'm okay." Said Rachel.

I blinked a few times over and over. I was taking it all in. The room. The condition of my beloved Rachel. Grace. The nurse taking care of her. It was all surreal. I was in disbelief. Rachel looked over in my direction with saddened eyes. The nurse had finished checking over her vitals and was taking the bladder full of the blackish fluid and discarding it in the wastebasket off in the far corner of the room. It was fluid being removed from her ports that Rachel had on her lungs.

"Miss Fairborn I'll be right outside if you need me. I'll come back in to check on your vitals in thirty minutes."

"Okay thank you, Hayley." Said Rachel to the nurse.

Grace ran up to her mom and gave her a gentle hug and laid the flowers down by her side. Grace was by no means immature in the situation. She knew what was going on. You could see it in her eyes. You could tell she knew everything that was taking place. Plus by the looks of it, being nine years old and the way she talked she didn't sound like a nine-year-old. Her heart belonged to her mother. As did her mothers. They embraced for several seconds before letting go of each other.

"Thank you for the flowers baby. Now I'll tell you what, why don't you let me and Lucifer talk, and I'll come call on you in a bit." She said.

Grace looked up at me and then back at her mother, then back at me.

"You like my Mom, don't you?" She asked.

I leaned down to become at eye level with her.

"I don't like your mother," I said.

Grace's little face was in disbelief.

Then I responded.

"I adore her," I said.

This made them both smile.

"I'm going to draw you a picture." Said Grace before running out of the room and down the hallway.

I chuckled a bit before looking back at Rachel. Rachel was rubbing her forehead looking at me. She had the slightest smile on her face. Her color had returned to her face, and she was studying the flowers that I had picked for her that Grace had given her.

"Lu. We need to talk." Said Rachel as she extended her shaking hand outwards placing the flowers on the immediate nightstand next to her.

"I know," I said.

"We need to talk about Grace." Said Rachel.

MorningStar Chapter 19

"She's mine isn't she?" I asked.

Rachel was quiet for several seconds before responding.

"Yes. In every way, she's yours." Said Rachel, now adjusting to where she was halfway sitting in the bed.

"I'm sorry. I didn't know. Otherwise, I would have–." I said before being cut off.

"I wanted to tell myself that a thousand times over. I wanted to tell myself that you had changed for the better. I had no way to contact you. No way to reach out." Said Rachel.

I was speechless.

"Lu. Everything about you is a complete chaotic mystery." She said while looking away from me.

"How am I to explain any of this to her? Where you've been. Who you are. And now you show up at my doorstep with flowers in hand when I'm dying." Said Rachel slightly coughing a bit.

I took a glance at her vitals on the monitor. Her oxygen was at 85%.

"I never meant to hurt you. That was never my intention." I said while taking a step toward Rachel's bedside.

"She's so smart. So incredibly talented. But there's something there." Said Rachel.

"Something there?" I said while sitting at her bedside next to her.

Rachel was now completely upright against her pillows. She wiggled her nose and adjusted the oxygen line pumping air into her nostrils.

"Yes, there's something otherworldly about her. Just like you."

The hairs on my arms stood up.

"Just like me?" I asked.

Rachel grasped my hand, staring deep into my eyes.

"She's blessed." Said Rachel as she rubbed the top of my hand. Her touch was cold.

"She's blessed?" I questioned.

Rachel's head slowly nodded up and down.

"She's an angel, Lu. Just like you." She said.

Yes. It's true. Rachel knew of my little secret. Obviously I couldn't keep it a secret from her after we had tousled the first time. But she accepted me for what I was. For who I was. At first it took some adjusting to get used to, but after that it didn't phase her. I was willing to take that chance of exposing myself in angelic form to her. Usually this meant dire consequences, as I've told you before. I didn't care. She unlocked parts of me I didn't know were locked. When we first made love, I thought I was going to be struck down and instantly shift and die. But it didn't happen. I was too caught in the moment to care anyway. I had always tried to wear something to confine my wings in front of her. She had always encouraged me to let my wings out.

Then the drinking started back up. I had apparently tried to expose myself to half the town of Haven during a fall festival. She did everything to try to discourage me from leaving that night. She knew. I had explained to her that if exposed, I'd die. I ended up passed out half way on the couch and half way on the floor. We didn't know why I could be exposed to her and nothing happened. I even asked Father on several occasions why it was okay. Although that channel of prayer to Father always seemed to go one way. I hadn't conversated with him since before I was kicked out of Heaven. Yes, the beauty of our relationship was like any other. A fallen angel that had fallen for a mortal.

"She's- She's just like me?" I said in disbelief.

"In every way." Said Rachel.

Rachel rubbed her forehead. You could tell that the coughing spell took a lot out of her.

"But. But how?" I asked.

"You tell me Lu. You tell me how." Said Rachel in an annoyed tone.

"I don't know." I said.

"Everything was fine up until this year. Up until the last few doctor's visits." Said Rachel now pointing at her own fingers.

"First it was the vitals. Her blood pressure was through the roof. Second, her heart rate was abnormally high. Third, was the wings." Said Rachel.

It was normal for an angel to have abnormally high blood pressure. A quick metabolism. A fast heart rate that would leave mortals in disbelief. And of course wings.

"She has wings!" I shouted, while covering my mouth realizing I had just shouted that.

"She has wings," I whispered in Rachel's direction.

Rachel nodded yes.

"For about three months now." She said.

"I got sick last month and have been trying to figure out what to do." Said Rachel.

As it stood. Rachel had no living family members. Not even a cousin or an aunt or uncle. Her entire family had passed on earlier in her life. At the age of fourteen she lost her father in a trucking accident. It was a tragic day for her. As for her mother she never really got to know her mother, just that one day she was there and the next she wasn't. She spent the remainder of her teenage years bouncing in and out of the system from family to family until she turned eighteen.

"Figure out what dear." I said as I took my finger and rubbed the side of her cheek with it.

She pulled my hand away.

"Lu. Look at me. Really fucking look at me. I don't have long, and she has nobody. I don't want her getting thrown into the system like I was." Said Rachel that had now had tears forming in her eyes.

"I'm going to fix you. There's got to be some way, somehow." I said. Rachel shook her head no.

"No." She said as she continued to shake her head.

"There's got to be someway I can fix you, I know there is." I said.

"Lucifer. I'm so afraid. I'm so fucking afraid, of what's going to happen when I'm gone." Said Rachel with tears now pouring down her face.

"We'll fix this. We'll find a way to fix all of this." I said.

"How? How are you going to fix it, Lu? How are you going to make it better? How are you going to—" Said Rachel, now obviously angry.

"By being a father to her." I said while interjecting.

"By what?" Asked Rachel.

" I mean I'm here now. I never would have left if I would have known, and you had no way to reach me all of these years. My point is.. My point is that I can be here now and help take care of you two." I said.

"Are you drinking?" Asked Rachel.

"Am I what?" I asked.

"Are... you... drinking?" She said this time slower.

"Honestly the last thing I drank was eight energy drinks and a coffee about two days ago." I said.

"That doesn't answer my question Lu." She said.

"Yes I've had a few but not much. The last drink I had was about a week ago in a bar in Nashville." I said.

I wasn't about to lie to her. Not her. I couldn't do that. I wasn't compelled to do so. She gave me a look as if she was about to say something about my last drink then stopped all together.

"Fine. But if you're staying you're staying for her." She said.

"If you want you can set up in the guest bedroom. There might be some clothes that fit you that Josh has left." She said.

I was a little puzzled by the comment.

"Who the hell is Josh?" I said.

Just then Grace came bursting in through the door.

"Josh is Mom's ex boyfriend. He doesn't stay with us anymore." Said Grace.

"How much of that conversation did you hear?" Rachel asked Grace.

"Just the last part about Josh, and how Lucifer can stay in the guest bedroom." Said Grace.

"Okay what did I say about listening to conversations." Said Rachel.

Grace traced her foot on the ground while putting her hands behind her back.

"Do not do it. Do not be listening in on other people's conversations." Said Grace.

Rachel had a stern look on her face toward Grace, before returning the same look back to me.

"Lucifer is in fact going to stay in the guest bedroom. Maybe you can show him where things are and where he will be staying." Said Rachel.

"Okay I can do that!" Said Grace, who was now grabbing my index finger and pulling me out of the room.

RACHEL SMILED AS I waved at her and exited the bedroom with Grace.

MorningStar Chapter 20

Trigger warning, this chapter contains talks of domestic abuse briefly.

GRACE LED ME DOWN THE hallway away from the bedroom Rachel was in.

She tugged on my fingers. Her grip was getting stronger and stronger.

"Come on this way!" She said.

She was eager to lead me down the hallway. We rounded the hallway and through the kitchen. There was a nice dining room table set up and the nurse was filling out some paperwork there at the table.

Grace pointed at a closed door.

"Here ya go," She said.

I opened the door to the room and was met with a simple queen size bed, two windows with curtains, and a box labeled "Josh". The sunbeams were blaring through the back window within the room. This meant it was nearly two or three just by the position of the sun.

"So Grace. Tell me about Josh." I said while turning the shutters to the closed position, where the sunbeams were coming through.

I was jealous. Jealous that someone else had been in my footsteps and gotten to know such a wonderful set of people. As for Grace, I didn't know if Josh had been a father figure or not to her. Was I a father figure to her? I had to earn respect from Grace.

"Josh was really tall. Like you. Everybody called him J for Josh. He smelt funny though, like a skunk most days. He'd come from outside and smell of it really bad." She said.

I assumed she was talking about the devil's lettuce. Weed.

"Well, that just sounds terrible," I said.

"Yeah, he had terrible taste in weed." Said Grace.

I was caught off guard. I wasn't sure what to say to her next, after that comment.

"At least that's what mom always said," Grace said.

"He did other drugs too, that Mom didn't like." Said Grace.

I studied the room briefly then shifted my attention back to Grace. She was rolling her shoulders forward and back. A sign of confined wings. She caught me looking at her making the adjustment in her shoulders and quickly looked away as if nothing was going on.

"Well, your mother is a brilliant woman." I slowly adjusted my shoulders as well.

My wings were slowly starting to bother me from being confined as well. You would think after flying all night that they wouldn't be. This caught Grace's attention although she didn't pick up on the fact that I was adjusting my wings. She thought that I was copying her.

I sat on the edge of the bed. While looking at the nightstand next to the bed that had a holy bible on it.

"Ah the NJV. The New King James Version." I said while picking it up

"You read?" Asked Grace.

"I dabble in scripture," I said.

"What about you?" I said.

Grace was abnormally tall for her age. About five foot four, from what I could pick up from looking at her. Her eyes were that of color like her mother's. Her hair was what could only be described as dirty brown. Shades of different brown streaked across her hairline.

"I dabble too. Sometimes I read revelations at night." She said.

"Ah, the vision from John of the coming days of the apocalypse," I said while shutting the bible.

"Yep, did you know angels are mentioned at least two hundred seventy-three times in the Bible?" She said joyfully.

I cleared my throat and looked her in the face.

"How do you know this?" I asked.

She shrugged her shoulders while sitting on the plastic tote labeled Josh.

"I just do, I've read lots of the bible. Some parts more than others." She said.

There was something she was clearly trying to ask me. I could tell by how she looked down at the ground and then back at my face.

"Lucifer, will you promise me something?" Said Grace.

"Maybe it just depends on what it is," I said, chuckling.

My laugh quickly went away as I realized that wasn't the response she was hoping for.

"Nevermind." Said Grace.

"No. Of course, I promise. I pinky promise, see?" I said while extending my pinky finger towards her.

She made eye contact with me, and then looked down at my pinky finger.

"Okay. You know how I saw you kissing Mom earlier right?" Said Grace.

"Yes." I said.

"I just know that's what adults do when they like each other. Especially the way you guys kept doing it, I could tell you both like each other." Said Grace now extending her pinky and locking it with mine.

"Go on," I said, listening intently.

"I just want to make sure you aren't like Josh. So do you promise you won't hit my Mommy?"

My heart sank deep into my chest. My gut was twisted. Did I really hear what I just heard? My pinky was still interlocked with Grace who was smiling at me with those pretty blue eyes of hers.

"Hit Rachel? I'd never." I said.

I quickly realized I needed to ask her more questions.

"When did this happen?" I asked Grace.

"Oh, it's been since mom has been sick. Maybe last week sometime. Mom was out of bed and he came over to try and borrow some more cash. He said he needed it to clean up his life. He'd stay with us after being out all night. When mom said that we didn't have the money, I heard a loud slapping noise from the kitchen. Mom was on the ground—." Said Grace, now with some tears in her eyes.

I was disassociating. The only thing I was feeling was rage. Pure chaotic rage.

"Mom was on the ground and then what?" I said as I stood up and cracked my knuckles.

I was fuming mad.

"Mom was holding her face, telling him to leave, and he kept shouting at her, calling her... calling her a..." She said as I helped wipe a tear coming from out of her eye.

"It's okay. You can say it," I said encouragingly as I tried to comfort her.

She took in a small breath and then made fists with both of her hands. She clearly was mad.

"He called her an ugly bitch. Over and over. And that nobody would love her." Said Grace.

"He only stopped shouting because I came into the room and gave Mom a big hug while she was down on the floor. She held me tight. I held her tight as well. The next thing I knew that happened was he was gone. We both heard the front door slam close and watched as he took mom's cash anyways and ran." Said Grace.

I rubbed my head and wanted vengeance for my Rachel. I needed to do something.

"Grace, I promise I will never ever do that to you or Mom as long as I shall live," I said while extending out my pinky.

She started to smile and connected her eyes with my face, wiping away the last remaining tear from her eyes.

"Pinky promise?" She said.

"Pinky promise." I said.

"Now I know we don't know each other that well, but I'm here to protect you and mom. You can trust me that I would never do something other than that of keeping you two safe." I said.

Words were just forming as I continued to speak. I was livid. I needed answers. I needed to know where Josh was.

"Now Grace. I need you to tell me where you think Josh is now." I said.

She looked at me as if her prayers had just been answered.

"Oh, I know exactly where he is," She said.

"Really?" I said.

"He's probably just down the street, getting high at the drug house, that's where he usually is when I ride by on my bike, during the day." Said Grace.

"Okay here's what I need you to do. I need you to tell me which house it is exactly without drawing attention to yourself. Could you point the house out to me as we drive by it?" I said.

"I can do that. It's not far from here.." Said Grace.

"You're not going to tell me no, or wonder why we're doing this?" I asked.

She rolled her eyes as if she already knew.

"I already know why Lucifer. You're going to kick his ass." Said Grace.

"Precisely my dear. Let's go get some ice cream" I said.

"Ice cream! I love ice cream!" Said Grace happily.

"But you have to make me a promise." I said.

Grace studied me briefly for a moment. The same way I studied mortals. It was bizarre, to say the least.

"What promise would that be?" Asked Grace.

I scratched the back of my head and squinted my eyes.

"Don't...tell...Mom." I said as I extended my pinky.

I was met with her pinky interlocked with mine.

"Promise." Said Grace, with her wonderful little smile.

MorningStar Chapter 21

Grace had left the bedroom to tell her mother that we were going to get ice cream. I heard the conversation from down the hallway.

"Mom, Mommy. Lucifer is going to take me to get ice cream!" Shouted Grace.

"Oh really?" Said Rachel.

"Where is Lu, right now?" Asked Rachel.

I was already headed down the hallway to Rachel's bedroom. I studied the family pictures of Grace growing up as I walked by them. There were beautiful pictures of Rachel as well. Some of them were taken in the springtime, while others were taken in the fall.

"Speak of the devil and he–" I said before being interrupted.

"Shall appear," Said Rachel with a saddened face.

She was cleaning her nose and eyes off. She had clearly been crying but hid it behind her smile. I looked at both of them with something that was in my heart that hadn't been there before. It wasn't always my intention to be a creature so full of sin and hate. But I had come to know what love was. I saw it between both of them. Rachel had always been a part of me, and she welcomed me back into her heart and home as if I had never left. It's as if all was forgiven. Did I honestly deserve to be loved by such a beautiful creature? And if I did, what was the cost associated with it?

"So you want to take Grace to get some ice cream?" Asked Rachel.

"Yes, if that's alright with you," I said.

"It's fine. But only to get ice cream. Nothing else." Said Rachel.

"Can I borrow your car?" I asked.

Rachel looked at me then back at Grace.

"What are you two up to?" Asked Rachel.

"Mommy, Lucifer wants to borrow your car so he can drive me to get ice cream." Said Grace.

"How did you—. How did you get here from Nashville?" Asked Rachel.

I cupped my hands together and then answered as honestly as I could with Grace in the room. It would go right over Grace's head anyways.

"I flew," I said.

Rachel's eyes became big.

"You flew. All the way from Nashville to Kansas?" She asked.

"Precisely," I said as I uncupped my hands.

Grace was listening intently to the conversation. As far as she knew I had flown in a plane. As far as it went with Rachel she knew exactly what I meant when I said "I flew."

"You can take the car, there's some money in my purse." She said pointing at her purse in the corner of the room on the dresser.

"Hooray! We're going to get ice cream!" Said Grace with excitement.

"I'll go get my shoes on!" Said Grace as she ran down the hallway and veered off to the right to a nearby bedroom door.

"Lu. Ice cream only. No funny business." Said Rachel.

"Business only got it," I said.

After all, taking care of business by surveying the drug house was part of my business. Josh had made it my business when he harmed Rachel and put Grace in the situation as well. Such actions like that made it all my business. Besides, all I wanted to do was talk to the guy a little.

"My keys are hanging up in the hallway. It's the only set of keys hanging up on the key rack thing," said Rachel.

"Can I—. Can I get another kiss from you?" I asked.

"Yes," Said Rachel.

I walked over to the bedside and leaned down to kiss her forehead. Before she grabbed my shirt and pulled my face down towards her lips. Her lips connected with mine. I gently closed my eyes as I enjoyed the moment. She was doing the same.

"I'm ready!" Said Grace from down the hallway.

I stopped kissing Rachel and pulled away slightly.

"Looks like that's my cue," I said.

"Looks like it," said Rachel.

"See you in a bit," I said.

I walked out of the bedroom, into the hallway where Grace was meeting me.

"You coming, Lu?" Said Grace.

"Yup just gotta grab the money and the keys."

"I'll grab the keys, you get the money then we can meet halfway." Said Grace.

"Sounds like a plan," I said.

I watched as Grace started to skip down the hallway. Her left wing had come undercovered slightly beneath the back of her shirt. It was a majestic white color. I could see the lush feathers that were coming down off of her wing, but just a portion of it. She needed to tuck her wings again before we went anywhere. But could I tell her? No. Not yet. All in due time. I quickly went back to the bedroom and Rachel could see the look on my face.

"What's wrong?" Asked Rachel.

I begin to whisper.

"Her wing is hanging out," I whispered to Rachel.

Rachel's look was that of disbelief. She quickly set up in bed.

"Grace, honey, why don't you come here real quick before you go." Said Rachel.

Grace came skipping back down the hallway. Pushing right past me to her mom.

"What Mommy?" Said Grace.

Her wing was still hanging out below her shirt. I couldn't help but study it. This child that we had created was a human. No, a hybrid. Part angel, part human. Grace was unique. She was perfect. That was my cue to step out of the bedroom while her mom had her fix the wing that was exposed. I went back towards the front door, where it opened back up to the kitchen on my right and the living room directly in front of me. The nurse was still busy with paperwork.

"Okay, Lu. I'm ready." Said Grace as she skipped down the hallway.

Her secret is safe with me, even though she didn't know I knew yet.

Her mom had clearly had her adjust her pants, and tuck her shirt in so that her wings would be confined.

"Let's go," I said as she threw the keys towards me and I caught them.

MorningStar Chapter 22

"Do we need to get your booster seat?" I asked Grace. She had a perplexed look on her face, as we walked outside to the car.

"Dude, I'm almost ten years old." Said Grace.

Her tone told it all she was not pleased with me asking this question.

I kneeled by her, looking at her directly to make eye contact.

"Look, I'm not very good at this," I said.

"What is this?" Asked Grace.

"You know, taking care of a child. I didn't know you didn't need your car seat," I said while opening the door to the car for Grace.

The car wasn't necessarily new, but it was well taken care of. It had to have been one of the early models of the Chevy Traverse. White was the paint color. With Grace inside the vehicle, she stopped me from shutting the door with her hand.

"Thank you for opening the door for me, Mom said you were always nice like that." Said Grace.

I leaned my head into the car where Grace was sitting.

"Did she now? What else did Mom say?" I asked Grace.

I was curious now. I wanted to know more.

"She said you and her used to date a long time ago." Said Grace.

Grace looked over my shoulder. A jet was flying overhead. She was studying it intently. I watched as she rolled her shoulders ever so slightly. Her wings were bothering her. So much so that she let out a muffled noise of pain.

"Ouch." She said, in a saddened voice.

The pain hit me as well, I could feel it in my wings. I would need to let my wings out soon to stretch out.

"Are you okay Grace?" I asked softly.

I was concerned. She was going through all these changes and had no one to turn to, other than her mother, Rachel. I mean was I father material after being gone all these years?

"I'm fine. I just—. I just moved the wrong way. I'm fine." Said Grace.

"You know there's a trick to that...Did you know that?" I said.

"Really, what's that?" She asked curiously.

I started to demonstrate.

"First you put your hands above your head," I said to Grace as I put my hands above my head.

She stretched out her small arms and hands and put them above her head.

"Like this?" She asked curiously, still trying to figure out how this was going to help out the pain.

"Precisely like that," I said.

"Are you ready?" I asked.

"Ready..." Said Grace.

With her hands above her head, I tickled her belly until she was full of laughter.

"Here comes the tickle monster!" I said.

"Stop. Stop. Stop. You're making me laugh Lu!" Said Grace.

Her smile was back. As was mine. I couldn't help but smile at this beautiful little girl.

"Any pain?" I asked as I stopped tickling her.

"No. None at all," She said, still giggling from all the tickles that she had just received.

"How about we go get that ice cream now?" I asked.

"Mint chocolate chip." Said Grace.

"Is that your favorite?" I asked.

"Yes. Mommy's is also—" Said Grace.

"Mint chocolate chip," I said.

I shut the back passenger door to where Grace was sitting. I went around the traverse, got in on the driver's side, and shut the door. I started the vehicle. I rolled the windows down so Grace could get some immediate air, before starting up the a/c. The smell of the pine trees that lined the driveway filled my nostrils.

"What's your favorite ice cream, Lu"? Asked Grace now buckled in.

I adjusted the rearview mirror so I could see her.

"My favorite is vanilla. Just plain, simple vanilla." I said while backing up in the driveway.

The crunching noise of pine needles could be heard as the car ran over them in different areas of the driveway.

I was by the mailbox at the end of the driveway. I could either go left or right.

"Grace, which way do you want me to go, right or left?"

I watched her in the rearview mirror as she pointed out toward the right.

"Go right." Said Grace.

"You know what we have to do before we go get ice cream right?" I asked her as I turned right.

"It's not that far from here. I know what we have to do, Lu. We have to kick ass." Said Grace.

"Grace. We're not kicking anyone's ass. I'm going to handle it. I'm just going to have a little one-on-one time with Josh."

"Don't lie to me." Said Grace.

"Don't what?" I said.

"Don't lie to me. You're going to kick his ass, I know you are going to. Don't treat me like a child." Said Grace.

I took a moment to clear my mind before responding. She was right. I was lying to her.

"Okay. You're right I am going to do very bad things to Josh." I said.
"Good. He deserves it." Said Grace.
"Yes, he does," I said while grinding my teeth.
It was an angry habit. Anytime I'd get angry I'd grind my teeth.
We traveled for another few blocks and a few turns left and then a right.
"There it is. That's the house right there." Said Grace.
Sure enough, just as I expected. A house with wooden siding pulled off in various places with a chain link fence around the yard. A sign was attached to the single tree that grew in the yard. "NO TRESPASSING" is what is read.
"So that's it. Who is that?" I asked Grace as I pointed.
Three men were up on the porch drinking and smoking, sitting in lawn chairs. One was taller than the other two men, he was the one standing. I drove by slowly as I came up to the house. I wasn't trying to draw attention to us, but I wanted a good look at the house and Josh.
"That's Josh. The tall one. I don't know who the other two are." Said Grace.
"Bunch of assholes by the look of it," I muttered under my breath.
Josh had his back turned towards me as we slowly passed by the house. It was only then that he had turned around. The tint on Rachel's car windows was dark enough that he couldn't make out who was driving. All I know is he knew it was her vehicle. His arms were tattoed up with various garbage. Done by a homemade tattoo gun. He wore a black beanie on top of his head and had some weird-looking facial hair going on. It was a failed attempt at a goatee. He flipped me off in my direction. Probably thought it was Rachel. He lifted his other hand, pulling up his shirt and exposing a black pistol that was tucked into his jeans. I was pissed.
But I wasn't about to do anything in front of Grace. Not now. She didn't need to see anything and I needed to get her out of harm's way. The radio in the car said 4:48 pm, the sun would be going down soon.

With my eyes on Josh, I drove by the house and continued, still looking at him, in the rearview mirror, while he stared back still giving me the middle finger and spitting on the ground. Vengeance was going to be mine. But first I had a promise to fulfill.

"I hate him." Said Grace.

"Me too," I said to Grace, as I gripped the steering wheel.

"Let's go get that ice cream Grace," I said.

"Yay, Ice cream!" Said Grace.

Morningstar Chapter 23

We pulled back into the driveway of the house. Grace got out of her seat of the car and rushed inside, while I followed close behind. The sun was nearly down. You could make out the different shades of colors among the clouds as the light was quickly disappearing. I took a moment to take in the beauty of the sky. I had made a little girl happy.

"Mommy Mommy. We got you your favorite." Said Grace as she ran down the hallway to the back bedroom where Rachel was.

"Did you now?" I heard Rachel say.

"We sure did. Mint Chocolate chip for my lady," I said as I handed Rachel her ice cream in a cup.

She gladly took it with a smile. Grace had got a double dip of mint chocolate chip on an ice cream cone. All I could think about was Josh. What a scumbag. What a pitiful waste of a creature. For him to hold that much hate towards Rachel and probably even Grace, to flip me the bird and show a gun off that he had, he had to be stopped. There was no way around that.

"I like this." Said Rachel.

"You like what?" Said Grace.

"Just this moment. Just the three of us all eating ice cream." Said Rachel as she ate a spoonful of her scoop of ice cream.

It was nearly dark. Rachel's condition seemed to improve for the moment. She wasn't in a coughing fit, and she was simply beautiful to take in. There were years I wanted back. Years that I couldn't turn back, because I wasn't here. Years I wasted in various bars, wandering from one city to the next. Nothing quite matched the feelings I had for her. She was my one. I had never fallen for another mortal since my existence. I was also sure I would never fall for another. Oftentimes I drank just to drown out the memories of being drunk instead of stepping up and loving her. It wasn't always that way, the problems started later in the relationship. Alcohol and I never mixed. Not only did it weaken my immortal state, but it also gave me alcohol neuropathy. Which felt like pins and needles stabbing me all over my body. It's more than likely from centuries of drinking. I deserved it after all. The slow tormenting feeling of my vessel slowly failing on me. Although if you recall I was drinking the night before I met Rachel at the coffee house. I should have quit then. But ultimately it was up to me to stop or not. But, you know who didn't deserve to be in pain? Rachel. She doesn't deserve any of this. By my hand, I will figure out a way to help her, no matter what that means.

"It's simply perfect," I said.

I turned to Grace and then looked back at Rachel.

"I think I could get used to ice cream nights," I said.

"Me too," Said Rachel.

"Me three," Said Grace.

The red numbered alarm clock on the nightstand next to Rachel's bed read 7:01 pm. I was assuming it would be Grace's bedtime soon. On top of that, I knew that Rachel would need her rest.

"Okay as soon as you finish up, you need to brush your teeth, and get ready for bed." Said Rachel.

"But, Mom." Said Grace.

"No, but's, brush those teeth and get that butt in bed." Said Rachel.

GRACE LOOKED UP AT me, you could tell she didn't want to go to bed yet. Probably a sugar rush. The sweets for angels could go one of two ways. Too much sugar and you could go into a sugar coma almost instantly. Too little and the effects would result in a spontaneous sugar rush. From bouncing all over the place to simply just being on edge.

"GoodNight Lu." Said Grace, as she stomped out of the room.

"Goodnight Grace," I said.

"You best drop the attitude, just as well." Said Rachel.

"You got a little firecracker on your hands there," I said while silently laughing.

Rachel's face was priceless. I knew exactly what she was fixing to say.

"I wonder where she gets it from," Rachel stated.

"Oh I can only imagine," I said as I chuckled.

I approached her bedside closer and sat down alongside her. I looked into her ocean-blue eyes as she looked back into mine. She softly caressed my face. I took the back of my fingers and rubbed along her jawline up to her lips. This made her smile even more.

"I missed you," Said Rachel.

"I've missed us," I said.

"You know, you're more than welcome to stay as long as you want. As long as you don't drink around me or Grace." Said Rachel.

"I think my drinking days have long passed me," I said.

"So what's your plan anyways?" Said Rachel.

"My plan?" I said.

"Yeah, I mean what brought you here? Why are you here?" Said Rachel.

I looked around to make sure no wandering eyes or ears were listening in.

"You want the truth. Okay." I said as I adjusted myself on the bed.

"The truth is I only learned yesterday that I had a daughter with the only woman I have ever loved. Gabriel told me yesterday in Nashville, that I had a daughter named Grace. So he must be keeping tabs on you from afar."

"Gabriel, your brother?"

"Yes. Stuff's been kinda all over the place as of late." I said.

She was curious. She wanted to know more.

"Not sure exactly what's going on. But Gabriel was supposed to fight me, on Dad's orders. He ended up self-sacrificing himself off a cliff into a watery depth. Then I went to go find Michael, to make sure he got to Gabriel in time, I ended up getting my ass kicked by him until I had enough. Then I ran into Raphael who told me some stuff I needed to do, then I ran back into Gabriel, and that's when he told me that I had a daughter. And now here I am."

Her eyes were big. She was shook.

"Are you alright?" I asked.

"It's just a lot to process all at once," She said.

"What's important is I'm here now," I said.

I reached my hand towards her hand and grasped it lightly. She grasped mine with what strength she had. She was getting tired, I could see it.

"If you're here, stay. If you're not going to stay then go," She said.

"Rachel. My darling Rachel. I'm not going anywhere." I said.

I stood up.

"But I ought to let you rest," I said with nothing more than vengeance on my mind.

She reached out to me.

"Can I get a kiss from you Lu?" Asked Rachel.

"Of course my darling," I said as I leaned in to connect her lips with mine.

She grabbed my face ever so lightly to keep my lips from leaving hers, then finally let go. She leaned in to whisper in my ear.

It was five words.

"Take care of our daughter." She said as she slowly became more lethargic.

It caught me off guard. She was right. If something happened to her, I would have to step up and take care of her.

"Goodnight my darling," I said as I exited the room and shut the door ever so quietly.

MorningStar Chapter 24

With the girls asleep I could leave quietly into the night. I carefully snuck out of the guest bedroom and into the hallway. I could hear the breathing of Rachel down the hallway, she was asleep. I couldn't hear Grace, however. I walked over to the front door and unlocked the deadbolt on the door. I did it as quietly as I possibly could.

"Where are you going?" Asked Grace from behind.

I didn't even hear her come up behind me. I struggled with the fact that I didn't hear her, come down the hallway or even remotely come out of her room.

"How did you do that?" I asked.

"Do what?" Asked Grace.

"How were you so quiet just now?" I asked.

"Sometimes I'm just super sneaky. Mom doesn't like it when I do it. I can be as quiet as a mouse is what she says. Anyways, where are you going, Lu?" She asked again.

"You know where I'm going," I said, as I turned around to face Grace.

"Oh. You're going to do it? Can I come with y–." Said Grace before I cut her off.

"No. Not only no, hell no. You're staying here." I said to Grace.

She stared at the ground for several seconds before looking back up to my eyes.

"But what if you need back up?" Asked Grace.

I was becoming slightly annoyed. I wasn't used to having someone try and tag-along. Especially that someone being my daughter. Hybrid angel or not, she could still get hurt, I wasn't about to take her around a bunch of thuggy crackheads. But I needed her to be confident in my abilities. I needed her to understand that everything was going to be okay. Then the thought occurred to me.

"I'll tell you what. I'm going by myself whether you like it or not. But I need you to do me a favor. Can you do me a favor while I go pay Josh a visit?" I asked Grace.

"Yes! What is it?" Asked Grace.

She was eager to help me in any way possible that she could.

"I need you to stay here, and make me a pot of coffee. Do you know how to make coffee out of the Keurig coffee maker you got there, in the kitchen?" I asked.

She was speechless for several seconds. She had a confused look on her face.

"Why do you need coffee, it's almost eight thirty pm?" She said while pointing at the clock by the front door.

"I just do, I promise I'll explain more when I get back if you're still awake." I said.

"So just one cup of coffee, I can do that." Said Grace.

"No. I need a full pot of coffee." I said.

She shook her head and moved her hands up by her face, she rubbed her forehead and looked up at me again.

"You need a full pot of coffee?" She asked.

"Yes, a whole pot." I said.

"Okay I can do that." She said as she went into the kitchen.

I followed her into the kitchen to see what she was doing. There was a little table set aside from the other counters, that was made up for just coffee and tea products. On it sat the coffee maker, along with a juicer and a toaster. There were different variations of coffee. She turned the button onto the Keurig coffee maker. Its color lit up blue, that illuminated on the kitchen walls.

"Now which one do you want, Lu?" Asked Grace.

"Whichever one has the most caffeine." I said.

She looked at the various bags of coffee grounds that were before us, studying each one carefully before selecting a single bag that read:

"Triple Shot Extreme".

"I think this is the one Lu," Said Grace.

"I think so too. Good job on finding it for me." I said.

"Do you want some coffee to take with you?" Grace asked.

"Absolutely. That is a fantastic idea Grace." I said.

We waited and watched as the coffee began to brew. She smiled in my direction and I smiled back in her direction.

"You're one of the good ones. I can tell." Said Grace.

"Oh, I don't know about that." I said.

The smell of freshly made coffee started to fill my nostrils. The slow drip of the hot liquidly deliciousness poured in front of my eyes.

"What makes you say that?" Asked Grace.

"I've just done a lot of bad things kid. I also haven't necessarily been there for ones that need me. In all honesty sometimes I think I'd be better off away from everybody. Because I feel different." I said.

"I feel different too. Ever since I—." She cut herself short.

"Ever since you?" I asked.

"Nothing. It doesn't matter. It's hard to explain." She said.

I knew she was referencing her wings. The fact that she had them. That would be a conversation for later to have with her. I didn't want to frighten her by telling her I also had wings. Or the fact that I was her father. All in due time.

"It's okay. You tell me when you're ready. Okay?" I said to Grace.

"Okay." She said.

The coffee maker beeped. My coffee was done. Grace had reached up in the cabinet and gotten down a thermos mug that was silver.

"This is mom's favorite thermos mug." She said.

"Don't lose it." She said.

"I'll try not to Grace." I said.

"So what's your plan?" Asked Grace.

"My plan?" I asked.

I took a sip of the coffee. I could feel the fast effects of the caffeine entering my bloodstream. It jolted me awake.

"Yeah, your plan. How are you going to kick Josh's ass?" She asked.

"Don't say ass." I said.

"Ass. Ass. As–" Said Grace.

"Alright. I get it." I said.

"Quit avoiding the question." She said.

Grace was in fact pretty grown up for her age. Her quick tempered personality reminded me of myself. I just wanted better for her. I wanted her to be better, and to have a better life. If father permitted her into existence, then it must have been for a reason. A fallen angel for a father, and a beautiful mortal woman for a mother. Here she was almost ten years old, without a father during that entire time. The only father figure she had during that time from what I could gather, was Josh. That wasn't a father figure. Not by a long shot. I would do right by her and Rachel too.

"I just plan on going in there, and talking to him and asking him for the money that he took from Rachel back." I said.

"You know he's not going to do it, right?" Said Grace.

"I know. I'm almost looking forward to it, Grace,if I'm being honest." I said.

"You want to fight him, don't you." Said Grace excitedly.

"Yes. Yes I do." I said while taking another sip out of the coffee mug.

"He disrespected you and Mom. Now he must pay." I said.

Grace was quiet again for several seconds, then hugged me. She came up to my chest, as she wrapped her hands around me. I carefully balanced the coffee in hand, as I was caught off guard.

"I like you Lu." Said Grace.

I patted her on the back with my opposite hand that wasn't holding anything.

"I like you too." I said.

She let go.

"Just promise me you'll be careful." Said Grace.

"I promise" I said as I held up my fingers and twisted them together, to show that I had crossed my fingers.

"You should get some sleep." I said.

"How am I supposed to sleep?" She said,

"Just go lay down, and close your eyes." I said.

"Will you tuck me in?" She asked.

This put a smile on my face. I had never tucked someone in before. I took it for what it was worth.

"Of course I will." I said as she led me to her bedroom.

Her room was pink. It had pink paint splashed onto the walls. Surrounding her bed was a pink see through cloth that had been hung from the ceiling. She jumped into bed. As she did this a small portion of her wing hung out, passed her shirt line. It caught me off guard again. Eventually we would have to have this conversation. One way or another it was going to happen. She needed to know that she wasn't alone. That even though she was different then everybody that she could at least look at me in the same light. Besides, it didn't seem to phase her. She seemed completely content in it.

"Well." She said to me as I took in her room and my surroundings.

"Yes. Time to tuck you in". I said.

I approached her bedside. She looked up at me with her beautiful blue eyes, that were very much like her mother's eyes.

I pressed in the sides by her feet, following along up to her shoulders, tucking her in, as I went.

"Now you're my little burrito." I said.

This had made her laugh.

"You're funny." She said, as she let out a big yawn.

She was drifting already. The time read 9 pm on her princess alarm clock, that she had on her nightstand next to her bed.

SHE TRIED TO FORCE her eyes to stay open as she muttered the last two words, before falling quickly asleep.

"Goodnight Lu."

I backed away from the bedside and turned out the overhead light in the bedroom.

"Goodnight Princess." I said quietly.

I made my way back to the kitchen and grabbed the thermos with the hot coffee in it that I had just been sipping on, and made my way outside. The cold night air filled my lungs. It wasn't too cold, but was cold enough to make one think that a light jacket might be necessary.

I started to walk. I walked until I was out of the driveway, and made my way towards the house I knew Josh was at. Grace was right. I did need a plan. I wasn't going to just go talk to Josh. A part of me couldn't wait to make him pay for what he had done.

Morningstar Chapter 25

I walked and sipped on the coffee that Grace had made me. The night sky was full of stars tonight. That was one thing I loved about the secludedness of Kansas. It was quiet, and most towns had communities that were spread out, which meant more light from the stars. You could make out the little dipper, Mars,and even Jupiter on a night like tonight.

I could hear the nearby barking of dogs as I walked along the pitch dark street. I was only a block away from the house where Josh had flipped me off earlier in the day and flashed his gun at me. In moments like this, I wished I had a little bit of nicotine to calm my nerves. Nicotine from tobacco didn't work very long. But it was something. I was more worried about how I was going to handle the overall situation with Josh. Not worried for my sake. But about how I was going to handle him. I wanted to hurt him. I wanted him to pay. I wanted him to know he couldn't do that ever again. Even If I didn't get the money back, at least I could make him understand that he could never touch or harm either of them again. I took another sip of coffee. I could feel the caffeine coursing through my bloodstream now.

There it was. The house. Littered with signs such as "Private Property", and "Do Not Enter." There was a fence that surrounded the small house that was falling apart. To the right of the front of the house was a tree. Upon that tree was a heavy bag that they had hung from a branch. There were lights coming from beyond the front door. A heavy thudding bass was hitting my eardrums and chest. Somebody beyond that front door, had music blaring. I opened the front of the fence up and shut it behind me. The loud thudding of the bass of whatever song was playing was getting faster. As for me, my blood was boiling. I was becoming enraged with each beat that hit my eardrums. I made my way up the steps and banged on the front door with my fist closed. The music continued. I could hear laughter coming from inside. Distant voices, each one at a different pitch being drowned out by this shitty music that kept blaring its bass.

I knocked again, this time pounding my fist on the front door, over and over.

"Who is that?" I heard from inside.

"Go check on it", Said another voice.

The music was turned down, almost completely. I could hear feet scramble each one of them at a different pace.

"Josh go answer the door." Said one of the voices.

"I got it. I got the fucking door, yall chill." Said what appeared to be Josh as feet approached the front door.

"Yo, who is it?" Said the voice from the other side of the door.

I made myself have a street accent and responded.

"Yo man it's Jeff. My boy said yall got the hookup. I need an ounce if yall got it." I said.

There was talking amongst them on the other side of the door. I could barely make out what they were saying.

"Ask him how much he's got on him," Said one of the voices from inside.

"How much do you got on you?" Asked the voice from the other side of the door.

I quickly blurted out a number that would be attractive enough to any drug dealer or tweaker.

"I got two grand on me yo," I said.

I hated talking like this. I found it stupid.

"This fool has two grand on him." Said the voice on the other side of the door.

I took the lid off of the hot coffee and threw the lid out in the yard.

"Get that cash off of him." Said one of the voices.

I had the coffee in my right hand.

The door started to unlock. Lock by lock it went until the door was open and Josh was standing in front of me. He had on the same clothes that he was wearing earlier. The only difference this time was that his pistol was in his hand.

"Give me that money you stupid mother fucker." He demanded

"You must be Josh, I said.

"What's that fucking matter. Cough up all that money you got on you, otherwise, I'll shoot you right here, right now!" He said as he brought the pistol up to my chest.

"I heard you like to hit women, Josh. We can't have that." I said calmly.

"Look bitch give me the money now or I swear I'll blow your head off right here" He said.

"This is what's going to happen. You're going to be saying sorry here in about five minutes." I said, as my blood started to boil.

I was becoming angry.

"The fuck I am bitch!" He said as he started to pull the hammer back on the pistol.

"Make it three minutes," I said as I brought my knee up into his crotch.

This made him drop the pistol out of his hand which I quickly kicked out of his reach. It slid off of the porch into the grass somewhere.

I then took what remaining hot coffee I had in the thermos, and splashed it onto his face. He screamed horrifically.

"Ahhh, my eyes! You fucking bitch!" He said while grabbing his face with his hands.

I snarled. I grabbed the back of his neck pulling his head up towards the sky and brought down my fist into the center of his face which caused him to collapse.

"What are you waiting for, get him!" Shouted Josh while crying under his breath in a ball at the doorway.

I kicked him in his ribs as I stepped inside the house and passed his body. Three guys looked up at me. The first one was tall. Just a little taller than me. He pushed past the guys that were getting up from the couch.

"I got this guys." He said to the two other guys that were now standing up off the couch.

"You better leave homie." He said to me.

"Or what?" I said.

He pulled out a full size pistol from the back of his jeans and unloaded a round into my side. It came out the other side, slicing through my flesh. Then he fired another round and missed. It hit the speaker system causing a spark. The noise from the gun echoed throughout the house. The ringing in my ears was more unbearable than getting shot at. Of course, there was blood coming out of my side, but just a little bit. I took three big steps toward him and grabbed him by his throat and picked him up off the ground. His legs were kicking frantically as he tried to break my grip, off of his throat.

All of the sudden one of the guys on the couch came up from behind me and swung an aluminum baseball bat upon my shoulders. Right when he did this motion the bat bent backward upon hitting my wings and sent a vibration up the bat, causing him to drop the bat. With the guy still in a choke hold in my grasp, I threw him violently through the drywall of the living room. The guy that had just hit me with the baseball bat, I picked up off the ground and headbutted as hard as I could. He slid for several feet, as he lay there on the ground.

"I don't want any trouble," Said the other guy who was still by the couch.

He was a skinny kid, that couldn't have been over eighteen if that.

"Good, cause I don't want any trouble either," I said as he studied the bullet holes that now had gone in one side and came out the other side.

My side where I had been shot made it mildly annoying to try to breathe.

"Right so let's see one down and out by the front door. One through the drywall, one down on the ground here" I said as I pointed at the guy I had just headbutted.

I snapped my fingers. Getting the attention of the kid by the couch. Clearly, he had been mixing with the wrong crowd. He had no business being in a house like this. He made eye contact with me.

"You will stay away from this house and will go home," I said.

"I will go home and stay away from this house." Said the kid.

"You will obey your parents and do good in school," I said while studying his eyes intently.

"I will obey my mom and do good in school." Said the kid, that was in a trance, frozen completely.

"Now get out of here," I said as I snapped my fingers.

The kid gathered up his bag and took off out of the front door. Never to be seen again. Josh had moved a little bit back into the inside of the house. He was still grabbing his face from where I had thrown the coffee directly at him and more than likely broke his nose.

"You're going to pay for this bitch." Said Josh, as I stood over him.

"If you come near me or Rachel, I'll put your ass in the ground, you got that?" I snarled into his ear.

"You're with that dying cunt? You can have that bitch and her piece of shit daughter." Said Josh as he went to reach for a knife in his pocket.

I grabbed his wrist and squeezed as hard as I could, forcing him to drop the knife out of his hand. I opened the knife up while holding his hand down onto the ground, and drove it through the center of his hand. He screamed with agony. I didn't care. He had set me off with his words. The noise of it driving through his skin into the hardwood floor was indistinguishable

"That's no way to talk about a lady, now is it Josh?" I screamed in his ear as I twisted the blade that was in his hand.

"No! No! It's not!" He screamed.

"Now say it!" I screamed into his ear.

"I'm sorry!" He said.

I twisted the blade again, blood trickled down onto the floor surrounding his hand.

"What are you sorry for Josh!" I shouted.

"I'm sorry for hitting Rachel!" He said.

"What else!" I said while twisting the blade in the opposite direction.

"I'm sorry for taking her money! I'm sorry for calling her a bitch!" He screamed in agony.

I let pressure off the knife I had been twisting into his hand. Sweat dripped off my forehead onto the ground.

"Josh, if I even so much as catch your shadow around my girls, or me, I'll shove this knife so far down your throat, you'll be begging for mercy. You got it?" I said.

"Yes– Yes– I got it. I got it man, just leave me the fuck alone!" Said Josh which was now grabbing his hand that was oozing out blood. It was still stuck against the hardwood floor.

A wad of cash was sticking out of the side of Josh's jeans. It was rubber banded together. There had to at least be a few thousand or so.

"I'll be taking this as well Josh," I said.

My breathing was becoming slightly shallow. My side, where I had been shot, was worrying me. I needed to make it back to the house. It was affecting my breathing.

I took in a deep gulp of air, and was met with blood coming out of my mouth.

"Who are you?" asked Josh as he tried to focus in on me, but couldn't on account of his eyes being burnt by the coffee I had thrown at his face.

I smirked as I walked over his body and onto the front porch.

"I'm the devil," I said while laughing and wiping the blood out from my mouth.

Down the block, I went. Back into the evening air, with a bullet hole in me and a wad of cash in my pocket.

I needed caffeine and I needed it quickly.

Morningstar Chapter 26

My shirt was covered in blood from where the bullet had hit me. At first, I thought it wouldn't affect me as badly as it did.

"Shit," I said as I inhaled while grabbing my side where I had been hit.

Yes, I know what you are thinking, aren't you immortal? The problem was guns and I didn't mix. Losing a significant amount of blood would drain me into a mortal state. Remember me saying only angels can hurt other angels? That wasn't necessarily the case when it came to guns if hit enough. With a caliber of a pistol like the one that was just used on me, I felt it.

The streets were quiet. The moon was illuminating the street I was walking down. The air was damp as if rain was coming in soon. It always had a certain smell in the air, right before it started to rain. I closed my eyes as I continued to walk forward. Step by step I went as my pace started to slow. In the distance was Rachel and Grace's home. I saw the light from the front porch from afar and was relieved. My heart was beginning to pound with each step I was taking. I unbuttoned my shirt and took it off. Sliding my arm out of the shirt on the side I had been shot on was extremely painful. It had hit me right below the second rib. I looked down at the damage as blood oozed out of the wound. It was far worse than I had thought. I tied the shirt around my waist with the main part of the shirt covering the hole in my side where the blood was coming out. It would help control some of the blood loss.

My wings shook. I stretched my wings out far and wide above my shoulders. I needed to get back to the house before I started to shift.

My heart was racing, if I didn't get caffeine in me soon I would shift and die. The shirt that I had tied around my ribs was already soaked in my blood. I had to try to fly towards the house. Nobody was in sight. I was still half a block out from the house. My vision was beginning to fade. I jumped up in the air and flapped my wings in a downward motion and hovered for several seconds before falling back to the ground. I caught myself on the ground. Loose little chunks of asphalt pierced the palms of my hands, where I had caught myself. I picked myself up with what strength I had left and kept shuffling my feet forward. Clearly flying was out of the picture. I could feel it. I could feel myself shifting. I neared the driveway. I reached out my hand for the mailbox but it slipped against it and blood smeared Grace's handprint on the mailbox. I had collapsed again, but this time my wings pierced the dirt in front of me, catching me from falling.

"Come on!" I said out loud to myself.

I dug deep. I thought about everything that I had done wrong. I thought about everything that I had done right. I thought about getting back to Grace and Rachel. I pushed up off the ground with my wings, which jolted me back to standing up. I shuffled up the driveway, with the front door just feet away from me. I walked up the front steps and fell to my knees. I was at the front door. All of a sudden the front door opened.

"Lu!" Said the voice as I faded in and out.

"Rachel, I'm sorry," I said as I kept my head down.

"You're a–. You're an angel!" Said the voice.

I coughed up blood and spit it out on the front porch to the side of where I was kneeling down.

"Fallen Angel," I said as I chuckled and looked up at what I thought was Rachel.

It wasn't my Rachel. It was Grace. She must have been staying up for me to return. My vision was still fading in and out. I saw the look on her face as she studied my wings as well as my condition.

"What do you need me to do," said Grace.

"Coff–. Coffee," I muttered as more blood came up out of my mouth.

Grace ran inside the screen door shutting behind her. I could hear her running inside. My head was pulsating. Everything was becoming blurry.

"Don't do this, Father," I said under my breath.

"I can't leave her," I said to the heavens.

The front screen door sprung open.

"Here! I got the coffee!" said Grace in a panic as she extended the entire coffee pot toward me.

I reached out for the coffee pot. It was cold to the touch. It didn't matter. Cold or hot, the caffeine from within would restore me, somewhat. I leaned back and lifted up my head towards the sky. With the coffee pot in hand, I opened up my mouth and tilted the spout into my mouth. The cold coffee ran down my throat as I gulped continuously. I felt the caffeine from within the coffee begin to course through my body. The cold liquid ran down my chin as I overfilled the capacity of what my mouth could swallow. I finished off the coffee in the pot within seconds.

"More," I said as I felt some of my strength return to me.

"Okay!" She said.

I extended the coffee pot up towards Grace, as she ran back inside to make more coffee.

I breathed, this time being able to breathe in without any sharp pain in my side. I had gotten the caffeine in me just in time. If it wasn't for Grace, I would have surely shifted and died. The shirt was soaked in my blood but it had prevented some of the blood loss. I chuckled.

"Must not be my time Dad," I said under my breath.

Several minutes had passed by before the screen door opened back up. This time Grace had another full pot of coffee.

"Here." She said as she carefully extended the coffee pot.

It was burning hot. Luckily for me, I didn't care. I opened my mouth wide as the hot liquid poured down my throat with each gulp. I stood up and continued to drink, with my wings stretched out above my shoulders. I felt the energy course through my bloodstream. I was healing. I was healing fast. I drank until every last drop was gone from the coffee pot.

"That's better," I said as I cracked my neck from left to right.

I untied the shirt along my ribs and let it drop on the front porch by my feet. I looked down at the damage, and to my surprise it was minimal. The blood had stopped oozing out of the wound, and the hole had shrunk down to the size of a dime.

"Lu. You're a–" said Grace.

"I am," I said.

Her face was in disbelief. She was speechless.

"I think you and I have a lot to talk about Grace," I said as I held out the coffee pot to her.

"More please," I said as she took the coffee pot.

Morningstar Chapter 27

She was confused. Hell, I would be too if a mysterious stranger that you had just met, turned out to have wings just like you. The only difference in our wings, from what I could gather was hers weren't black like mine, they were white as snow. She had her momma's looks and her daddy's wings.

"Are you okay?" Said Grace as she took the coffee pot out of my grip.

She wasn't even concerned about my wings. She was only worried if I was okay.

"Never better. You just make me more of that delicious coffee and everything will be okay." I said.

"But—. But why coffee?" Said Grace confusingly.

I scratched the top of my head knowing I had a lot to explain to Grace. It needed to happen. After all, it was the least I could do. She had just saved my life. If she had gone to bed and she wasn't there at the front door to greet me, I would have surely shifted and died. I stood up, looking around at the nearest neighbor's house. I was making sure nobody had seen me in this form, other than Grace. How do you honestly explain an over-six-foot man with black wings standing on a porch in the middle of the night? The wind blew slightly, cutting ever so sharply against my now almost healed wound along my ribs. Grace looked down at the shirt, covered in my blood, and then back at my wings.

"The coffee helps me. It's a healing factor. It's not necessarily just the coffee, it's the caffeine from within the coffee that speeds up the repair process of my vessel. The more caffeine I consume the faster the healing process." I said while cracking my neck from left to right.

We were still on the front porch. The moonlight shimmered through the evergreen trees in the driveway. All was quiet, all was still.

You could see the wheels spinning in her head. She still had questions that needed answers.

"Did you go see Josh? She asked already knowing the answer.

I reached into my pocket, pulled out the wad of cash I had taken from Josh, and handed it over to Grace. I nodded my head up and down.

"Josh won't be bothering you or Mom, ever again, I promise," I said.

She studied the money and then took a step forward. She was still within reach but was keeping her distance.

"Did you–. Did you kill him?" Grace asked.

"No. Not my specialty. But, I did make him suffer." I said.

I cleared my throat of the remaining blood and spit it out into the grass off of the porch.

"You make sure Mom, gets that money," I said.

"Where are you going?" She asked.

"I'm not going anywhere, I just want you to make sure she gets it," I said.

I looked over my shoulders, my wings were restless. They needed a stretch. I stretched them far and wide. As wide as I could. I looked down at Grace, her face was in awe.

"Be not afraid," I said.

"I'm not afraid, Lu..." Said Grace.

"We need to go inside," I said.

Grace opened up the screen door with the coffee pot in her other hand and stepped out of the way, while still holding open the door.

She was quiet about opening the door, the creaking of the screen door could be heard all throughout the house and out onto the front porch.

I stepped inside while lowering my wings so they didn't catch the door frame.

"I'll make you some more coffee." She said while quickly rushing into the kitchen.

"I'm going to get myself cleaned up," I said while walking down the hallway to the guest room.

"Okay, I'll bring you a cup once it is done," Said Grace.

My wings shuffled against the walls of the narrow hallway. I brought them in as far as a could so I didn't knock off anything that was hanging on the hallway walls. I entered the guest bedroom and set my eyes on the box of clothes with the label "Josh" was. I took in a deep breath and exhaled. I was feeling much more like myself. The healing nearly tripled with caffeine. In whatever form caffeine could come in. After almost two pots of coffee, I was feeling it. I started shuffling through the box. An extra large black hoodie caught my eye. I threw it on the nearby bed with some boxers and socks as well. As for pants, I found some jeans that looked like they would fit me and grabbed them from the box. I needed a shower. I smelled horrifically unpleasing. I gathered up the clothes from the bed with the jeans and made my way back down the hallway. I quietly shuffled my feet so as to not disturb Rachel. The last thing I needed was for her to wake up and see me in this condition or learn what I had done. I was nearly back in the kitchen where Grace was pouring me a cup of coffee.

"Here ya go." Said Grace as she handed me a cup of coffee.

She looked up at me with her beautiful blue eyes. It's as if I was in a trance for a spilt second as I gazed deep into her eyes. I quickly shook my head.

"How is any of this possible?" Asked Grace.

I sighed and took a sip from the coffee.

"There's so much I have to tell you, Grace," I said while taking another sip from the coffee.

She was studying my wings. I could tell on account of every time I shuffled slightly she watched them intently.

"But there's something you also need to tell me isn't there?" I said to Grace.

Coughing could be heard down the hallway. It was Rachel. She was coughing in her sleep. We both looked at each other and paused, as if we were both completely frozen, like statues. The coughing passed and we both took in a breath of relief.

"What do you mean there's something I need to tell you?" Said Grace.

I rolled my eyes ever so slightly. She was a tough case. Not only could she almost put me in a trance, but she was also good at keeping secrets. I sat the coffee down on the table.

"Come on Grace. I knew the moment I laid eyes on you." I said.

She took a few steps back toward the wall of the kitchen that was bare.

"I don't know what you are talking about." Said Grace now slightly defensive.

"Fine. I'm going to go take a shower. It's One-thirty-five in the morning, I suggest you get some sleep and maybe we can talk in the morning." I said in a stern tone while looking at the time on the oven display screen.

She stood her ground. She didn't like that tone coming from me.

"Yeah well, who are you to tell me to get some sleep? Talking to me as if you are my father?" She said loudly.

I put my finger up to my lips to tell her to be quiet.

"Shhhhhh. Shut it." I whispered.

"You're going to wake up your mother," I said.

Grace crossed her arms, and took a step toward me.

"Good. Maybe she needs to be awake. Maybe she needs to see that you have these huge black wings," Said Grace.

I sighed again while facepalming.

"Grace—. Grace listen—. She knows. She knows of me having wings. She knows every part of me. The good, the bad, the dark, and the light." I said.

I sat down at the kitchen bench taking another sip of the coffee.

"You see Grace—," I said while pausing.

She took another step toward me.

"Tell me, Lu. Tell me the truth." Said Grace.

I cleared my throat.

"Ten years ago, your mother and I were together. Nothing could separate us." I said while choking up on my own words.

Tears were beginning to form in Grace's eyes and mine as well. I looked down toward the ground and studied it for several seconds.

Just then a noise could be heard coming down the hallway to the kitchen.

It was Rachel hooked up to her IV on rollers.

She looked at both of us and without hesitation said:

"And now here we are ten years later Grace. You know who Lu is." Said Rachel while holding onto her IV roller.

Grace looked at her mom and then back at me.

"Who—. Who are you?" Said Grace.

I looked her in the eyes.

"I'm your father," I said.

Morningstar Chapter 28

Grace looked at Rachel, then back at me. The look on her face was that of confusion.

"But how can he be my–." Said Grace.

Rachel interrupted.

"You know how." Said, Rachel.

Rachel was leaning most of her weight on her IV roller, which was supporting her.

Grace looked back at me again tears rolling down the side of her cheeks. She was backed up against the wall of the kitchen.

"You're my–. You're my–." She said, choking up on her words.

I leaned down towards her putting my right arm on her shoulder.

"I am. And I'm so incredibly happy to finally meet you, and be a part of your life." I said as I gently smiled at her face that was looking back at mine.

"Dad–. You're my Dad?" She said while clearing the tears from off of her face.

"Yes, babygirl. I'm Dad and I'm so sorry for not being here sooner." I said.

"I wasn't aware that you even existed until about three days ago." I said in a saddened tone.

Grace's gaze switched from me leaning over her to her mother.

Rachel threw her hands up as if signifying a shrug of some sort.

"And I didn't know how to get ahold of him. I didn't know where he was. Or if he was even alive for that matter, so I kept it from you. I'm so sorry sweetie. I was just trying to protect you." Said Rachel who was now also crying.

Grace took a deep shallow breath. She was clearly internally freaking out.

"So you just screw my mom and run off and don't think for one second that maybe you should stick around for her sake or mine!" Yelled Grace as she glared into my eyes.

"No. no. no. I didn't know any of this would be possible." I said.

Rachel cleared her throat.

"He didn't know I was pregnant with you and he and I had a falling out." Said Rachel.

"You see Grace, Angels aren't supposed to be–. How do I put this?" I asked while looking in Rachel's direction.

"Angels aren't supposed to be able to have children." Said Rachel as bluntly as she could.

"Exactly," I said while still comforting Grace with my arm extended out onto her shoulder.

"Fine. So let's say all this is true. Let's say you are my Dad, and Mom didn't know how to get ahold of you. Why now?" Said Grace.

"Why now, what?" I said.

"Why are you here now? What made you decide to come now?" Said Grace.

I looked over at Rachel and then back at Grace.

"My brother," I said.

"Your brother?" Said both Rachel and Grace at the same time.

"Yes. Gabriel. Your uncle." I said.

The girls were both confused at this point. I had brought up Gabriel on rare occasions to Rachel but not a whole lot during our relationship.

"Gabriel as in the angel, Gabriel?" Asked Grace.

"Yes. That'd be the one. The last couple days have been hard to piece together, but he told me about you, Grace. He told me about you and I immediately flew here from Nashville." I said while exhaling.

The wound had closed up entirley but the pain was still there from being shot.

"Mom I'm so confused." Said Grace to her mother.

Rachel stood upright off of her iv roller and made eye contact with Grace.

"I'm so sorry princess. You were a miracle when you were born." Said Rachel.

I waited for my turn to talk. I could tell there was going to be more Rachel would say.

"To be honest, for the both of you. I don't have much longer. I have to tell you the truth, Grace." Said Rachel before letting out a deep raspy breath as if she was trying to catch her breath.

Grace's eyes begin to weep. Tears started rolling down her cheeks.

"What do you mean by that, Mom. You are going to beat this, I know you can, you can do anyth–." Said Grace before being interupted by her Mom.

"No. No I can't do this anymore. I'm so tired baby. The doctor's got my cancer cell count two days ago and called me this morning. It's spreading again. They gave me days. Not weeks, not months, not years, but days," Said Rachel.

The tears were now coming down one right after the other. Both of them were crying in a equal manner.

"You! You did this to my mom!" Said Grace while pointing the finger at me.

"I know you're upset Grace, but I did no such thing." I said.

"You broke her heart." Said Grace to me.

Grace was now standing up pointing her finger at my chest poking me repeadtly over and over.

"It was never my intention to break her heart." I said softly.

Rachel put herself between Grace and I. She pushed out her hands looking at the both of us.

"Both of you need to stop. This isn't helping anything. Grace, Lu never broke my heart. He mended it in ways that I never knew were possible. He made me fall for him time and time again as our relationship grew. Don't blame him for my cancer. It's not his fault." Said Rachel now too exhausted to hold her hands up any longer.

"Now wipe those tears away and the both of you listen to me. Lucifer is your father whether you like it or not. Plain and simple. He has wings and you have wings! And yes he already knows all about it. He's here because he just found out about you, and he had no idea that I was dying!" Said Rachel sternly.

Rachel turned her eyes to me and pointed at me.

"And you! I don't know what you were doing tonight, that caused all this?" Demanded Rachel in a sharp tone.

My wings slowly raised up and down. No other mortal could do this to me but Rachel. It was a sign of nervousness. I felt like I was backed into a corner.

"I was just trying to help." I said calmly.

"By doing what?" Said Rachel.

Grace held up the wad of cash to Mom.

"Here Mom." She said as she handed the cash to Mom.

"What did you do?" She snarled.

"I handled it." I said.

"Josh won't be bothering you two ever again." I said.

"So violence just solves all the problems does it Lu!" Yelled Rachel.

"Rachel no. Only to those that need to pay for the suffering of others. If they make someone suffer then they in return should pay for what they have done." I said.

Grace's face looked concerned for the both of us.

"Mom I told him all about Josh. I told him everything. Josh wasn't good. He deserved whatever Lu did to him." Said Grace.

Rachel turned her gaze from Grace back to me.

"And what exactly did you do to him?" Asked Rachel.

"I hurt him. I royally whooped his ass." I said.

Grace's attitude was changing. Rachel was starring at the wad of cash in her hand.

"This is way more then what he took from us Lu." Said Rachel.

"Then consider it interest." I said.

"He whooped his ass Mom." Said Grace.

"Language!" Said Rachel.

"Sorry Mom." Said Grace.

"Also, he got shot. He got shot right there." Said Grace while pointing at my healed wound.

"Oh my dear lord!" Said Rachel.

"I'm fine love. I'm fine." I said trying to reassure Rachel that everything was okay.

"You're an idiot." Said Rachel.

Everything was quiet for several seconds. It was late. Real late. I still needed to shower and Rachel needed her rest.

"Look I'll take the money. But you're still stupid to have gone over there and handle it. You could have gotten seriously hurt! I don't even know what you were thinking." Said Rachel.

I thought for several seconds before responding.

"I just wanted to keep you two safe." I said.

The eye roll was starting. Rachel rolled her eyes.

"Fine. Thank you. It's late, I'm cranky. Everybody needs to get their asses to bed. But first you need to go shower." Said Rachel as she threw a towel from the kitchen table at my chest.

I caught it in the air.

"Grace do you have anything else?" Asked Rachel.

"Not really other then I don't want to lose you mom. I'm scared." Said Grace.

"Listen to me. I'll always be with you no matter where I am in your life. Whether that be alive or dead, a piece of me will always be with you in your life." Said Rachel while extending out her arms for a hug from Grace.

They embraced for what seemed like minutes. I watched them both intently. The pain was nearly gone from where I was shot. The healing process was nearly complete. My vessal was going to be just fine, thanks to Grace.

"I love you Mommy." Said Grace while looking up at her Mom.

"I love you too." Said Rachel.

They had both almost completly forgotton that I was standing there.

"Grace let's get you in bed." Said Rachel.

"Okay Mom." Said Grace.

I smelled the fragrance off of the fresh towel that was handed to me. It smelled like lavender and other floral fragrances.

"And you." Said Rachel.

"You go shower." She said eyeballing me up and down like I was a meatstick.

I knew exactly what that meant. She wasn't mad at me. She was quite frankly wanting a piece of me. And that, that was okay to me, because I wanted a piece of her.

MorningStar Chapter 29

The next morning I woke up feeling refreshed. From the shower and other things of course. I didn't wake up of my own accord. I woke up to fingers rubbing my chest, up and down. I opened my eyes to Rachel lying next to me in the guest bedroom. Everything came rushing back to me. Sleeping wasn't a normal habit for angels. But deep meditation could be reached with practice. It was more like a sensory thing. I could turn off certain senses with enough practice.

"Good Morning Lu." Said Rachel in a playful manner.

"Good Morning Love," I said while stretching my arms out.

My right-wing brushed against her face and her shoulder blade ever so softly. At that moment all was silent. The only thing I could hear was the beating of her heart. It was pure bliss. She studied my eyes for several seconds while laying on my chest with her arms crossed.

"I need you to do something." Said Rachel.

I studied her for several seconds as well. Her frail body had been tormented by the chemotherapy. Her hair was completely gone. I remember her as if it was yesterday in the coffee shop, with her long flowing hair and beautiful smile.

"What do you need me to do my love?" I asked.

She had a big grin on her face. Whatever it was she found it humorous.

"I need you to take Grace shopping." She giggled.

"Shopping for?" I replied.

The giggling continued.

"I need you to take her shopping for sports bras." She said.

I sighed.

"She needs them. Her wings are only going to get bigger and she needs to be covered up for the most part as she continues to grow." Said Rachel.

"I'll do it," I said to her.

The giggling had subsided, and in place of it was a simple genuine smile.

She gently caressed my face with her small cold hand and rubbed her palm against my stubble in a small circular motion.

"Thank you, Lu." She said.

"It just makes sense that I start helping out around here with things," I said.

"You're the best." Said Rachel.

"What time is it?" I asked.

She looked over at the red glow of the clock on the nightstand. It was one of those older models with a radio feature.

"It's a quarter after eight am." She said.

"Shit," I said.

"What? Have some place to be?" She asked.

I sat up in the bed. Putting my back and wings against the headboard of the frame.

"No. Not at all. It's not that. I just didn't know if you wanted Grace to see–." I said.

"To see us in bed?" Said Rachel.

"Yes. Precisely." I said.

Rachel looked over at the door, then back at me with a devilish grin.

"You know she's probably still asleep after last night." Said Rachel.

"Yeah. You're probably right. But I should get up for the day and get halfway decent." I said while trying to sit up on the edge of the bed.

I was stopped. Rachel grasped my wrist and kept me in the sitting position still against the headboard.

"Where do you think you're going." Said Rachel.

I caught on. I knew what she was wanting. She instantly got my interest.

"I suppose I'll just stay right here," I said while looking her up and down.

Her half-naked body rubbed against me ever so softly and my senses were instantly heightened. I let out a mild growl. It was something I did when I was, how do I put this? Horny.

"Shhhh," She said as she held a finger up to her lips.

She started to kiss my neck.

KNOCK KNOCK KNOCK

Loud knocking could be heard coming from the door to the bedroom we were in. I scanned the room briefly as if I was on alert mode.

"Mom? Lu? Are you in there?" Said Grace from the otherside of the door.

Rachel wasn't stopping. I tapped her on the shoulder to get her attention. She was hyper-fixated.

"Yes. I'm in here." I said quickly.

I was completely embarrassed. Not only was Rachel in the room but she wasn't stopping what she was doing!

"Have you seen Mom?" Asked Grace impatiently.

I wasn't about to lie to her. Not her. Rachel needed to stop and get dressed it was as simple as that.

"Yes, she's in here," I said.

"Well, could you wake her or whatever?" Said Grace.

Rachel paused and smiled at me.

"I'll be out in just a second sweety. Lu, and I are just talking about some things."

"Okay." Said Grace as her voice begin to fade.

The pitter-patter of footsteps started to get distant down the hallway.

Rachel was looking up at me from under the covers, grinning that devilish grin again.

"Now where were we." She said.

I had no choice in the matter. It was pretty clear I wasn't going anywhere.

MorningStar Chapter 30

9:00 am is what the little alarm clock read in it's reddish glow that illuminated from the nightstand. I was relaxed. Rachel had gotten up and dressed and went to take care of Grace. She had left me to attend to my needs in the bedroom. Although she had covered one of the needs. I needed to get dressed. I sat up glancing over at the window blinds that were slightly shut and looked out the window. A cardinal had come to visit on the window ledge. A sign of a passed loved one or spirit coming to protect you. It was a legend as old as time itself.

"Hey, little guy," I said as if the red cardinal could hear me.

The bird stayed perched for several seconds before flying off.

I needed coffee. I needed a substance of some kind in the form of caffeine. I wasn't hurting anymore. My vessel was self-sustaining. It took care of itself in the long run. Rachel was right though. I could have been seriously hurt and was. If it wasn't for Grace and her amazing coffee-making abilities when I got back to the house, I would have surely shifted and died. But none of that mattered now. What mattered now, was shopping.

I peered over at the box of clothes that Josh had left and Rachel had marked with a permanent marker, "Josh's Clothes." I sorted through the box until I found a plain white tee and a pair of weathered jeans. Also in the box was a pair of square-toe boots. Steel toes as a matter of fact.

"Shit kickers," I said while holding up the boots and checking the tag for the size of the boots.

Size thirteen is what they read. Perfect size for me. I got dressed and headed down the hallway in my newly acquired clothes and boots.

One thing you got to understand is my ability to retract my wings at will. I couldn't necessarily retract them all the way, but I could do my best to tuck them into whatever clothes I was wearing. It was important that no other mortals other than Rachel and Grace saw me in my angelic form. The consequences could be dire. The smell of bacon filled my nostrils. A crackling noise could be heard. Grease was popping in a small frying pan that Rachel was standing next to.

"Good Morning Lu." Said Grace from the table. She was coloring in one of those adult coloring books with colored pencils. This particular drawing was that of a very detailed owl.

"Good Morning, Grace," I said.

"Mom told me you weren't feeling good this morning." Said Grace.

"Did she now?" I said.

"But she gave you medicine and made you feel better." Said Grace.

I cleared my throat as if I had just choked on my own spit.

"He's still a little stiff and sore. Said Rachel while winking at me from the stove.

She was cooking bacon and eggs.

"Have a seat at the table." Said Rachel pointing at the table with a spatula that was in her right hand.

"I saw a cardinal this morning," I said loud enough that both of the girls could hear me.

Grace stopped what she was doing with the coloring book and looked up at me.

"It sat for several seconds on the window ledge in the guest bedroom."

Grace started to speak.

"Mom told me that cardinals are a sign of a passed loved one coming to visit you. Or a guardian angel coming to protect you and check in on you."

"That's right," I said.

"Breakfast will be ready shortly." Said Rachel as she made her way over to the table.

She had a pep in her step. She was definitely in an elevated mood.

"Mom is having a good day." Said Grace.

"So am I," I said while leaning in over the table to look at the progress of the owl drawing she was working on.

"Me too." Said Grace.

"Grace, get everybody a fork." Said Rachel as she turned off the burner on the stove.

Grace got up from the table and went over to a nearby drawer passed the island within the kitchen. The clanking of silverware could be heard.

Rachel had started platting food.

"Before you run off give this to Lu." Said Rachel while extending out a plate of eggs and bacon to Grace.

Grace made her way back to me with three forks and a plate of food.

I extended my hands out to meet hers

"Here ya go." Said Grace.

"Thank you, dear," I said.

Rachel made her way with the two other plates of food to the table and sat down.

"Coffee is over there, Lu." Said Rachel.

She handed Grace a plate of food and sat the remainder of the food in front of her.

I got up and poured myself a cup of hot coffee and sat back down.

"So, I was talking to Grace about what we talked about earlier. About you taking her to the store to go shopping." Said Rachel.

"Yes," I said while shoveling food into my mouth.

She took the rubberband off the wad of cash I had given her and laid down a few twenty dollar bills, next to my coffee.

"This should be more than enough." Said Grace.

I put a couple of the twenty dollar bills into my pocket.

"So you're going to take me to get bras?" Asked Grace.

"Yes. Also, I think we should get ice cream as well." I said to Grace and Rachel.

"Good Idea Lu." Said Grace.

Rachel cleared her throat.

"Are you okay Mom?" Said Grace.

You could see it. That burst of energy she had was instantly gone. Nothing was left but pain and discomfort and fatigue.

"I'm just really tired guys." Said Rachel.

I finished up the last remainder of my coffee.

"What time does the home health nurse come to check in on you?" I asked.

"A few hours. Usually around noon." Responded Rachel.

Grace and I were both looking at her intently.

"I'll be okay guys. Quit looking at me like that." She snapped.

"Sorry," I said.

"Sorry," Said Grace in the same tone.

Grace had made eye contact with me and briefly smiled, before eating a strip of bacon.

"I'm going to go lay down. The keys are hanging up by the front door. Take her to the consignment store at first. And see if that works. Grace take your cell phone in case I have to get ahold of you, and tuck in your wings." Said Rachel.

Rachel made her way down the hallway to the room with her medical bed in it.

"Love you guys." She said.

"Love you too," I said, as did Grace.

The door shut to her bedroom and coughing could be heard coming from the other side.

"You about ready?" I asked Grace.

"Ready!" She said excitedly.

MorningStar Chapter 31

We were nearly across town, just a few more minutes in the car and we'd be at the store. I had Grace ride up front with me. It was nice, just her and I. The radio was playing some old country hits according to the DJ. We passed the coffee house where I had met Rachel.

"Look Lu, that's where Mom used to work!" Said Grace excitedly.

"That's actually where I met your mother about ten years ago," I said.

"Really?" She said looking over at me.

"Really, really," I said.

There was a grocery store coming up on the left side of the road. It was a rather small parking lot. I was studying a cardinal that was perched up on the grocery store sign. It hopped around and turned its head sideways as we passed it.

"Did you see–?" I said.

"The cardinal?" Asked Grace before I could say it.

"Yes," I said.

"They are always around me." She said while studying the floorboard of the car.

"The cardinals are always around you?" I asked.

"Mom said it's my good luck charm. To be blessed with so many guardian angels." Said Grace.

I was discouraged to say anything negative. We shared a moment of silence before I responded.

"Mom is pretty smart you know," I said while looking over briefly at Grace.

"Turn here Lu." She said as she pointed right at the next incoming intersection.

There was a mural on the side of a brick building and a small park beside that mural.

The mural was a painting of a man and a small child holding hands with a sunset in the background.

"This is one of my favorite places to go to. Mom and I used to come here for ice cream all the time. We'd sit at that bench right there." Said Grace.

It wasn't one of those large parks. It was just a small park with a few benches in between two brick buildings. It had a small fountain between the benches that was spraying out water. It was peaceful to look at.

"That sounds nice kiddo, real nice," I said.

"Mom and I haven't gone in a long time though, not since she got sick." She said in a sad tone.

I could tell this bothered her. In fact, I could feel her emotion. One of the things about being immortal is we could feel mortal's emotions sometimes. Even to the point of hearing their thoughts sometimes. I felt a deep sadness overwhelm me. Yes, the daughter of darkness was a hybrid. Half Human. Half angel. But the emotion and connection she felt for her mother was like no other. I could feel the heaviness in her heart. She loved Rachel dearly. As did I. The sadness was that of something I had never felt.

"Maybe we can go sometime? All three of us." I said.

"I'd like that Lu." Responded Grace.

It was silent again. Something was on her mind. I could sense it.

I looked over at her she was staring out the window as we drove by all the little brick-and-mortar shops.

"So what's on your mind?" I asked.

She let out a deep sigh.

"I don't know how to say this. Or what words to use for that matter." She said as she continued staring out the window.

She put her hands down on her thighs. Cleary whatever it was, was bothering her.

"I know this much. I know your my dad. But I don't understand how all this works. I've never had a Dad before, then suddenly you show up out of nowhere and–." She said as she started to sob suddenly.

I listened intently. I had never experienced this part of emotions from a human. In this case a hybrid. Part of me and part of the mortal realm. Stuck in between two worlds she had yet to even understand. It hurt me to try to even begin to understand just what she must have been going through for the last nine years without me.

"And you just come into our lives without even knowing about me. Mom told me you flew all the way from Nashville. I wanted to be angry at you for so long. I wanted to say the meanest nastiest things to you Lu. I wanted to blame you for all the years of you not being in my life." She said as she wiped the tears from her face.

We were nearing the thrift store. Just a little bit further and we'd be at our destination. I was frozen though by her words. All I could do was grip the steering wheel a little bit tighter and keep my eyes forward. Yes, I the "Prince of Darkness" was capable of feeling emotions. I just didn't want to weep, not now, not in this moment with Grace.

"But now that you're here, I don't want you to go. I feel this strong connection towards you." Said Grace.

"I feel it too Grace," I said without skipping a beat.

We had pulled into the thrift store parking lot. A low-lit sign overhung above the storefront. Jackie's apparel is what the yellow sign read above the thrift store entrance. People were coming and going with large bags of clothing. I put the car into park and stared over at Grace. I had to tell her how I felt. Now was the time to be not only a listening ear but to step up and be her father.

"You know Grace. Life has been weird." I said while glancing over at her and turning the car radio to mute.

"I don't expect you to understand or even accept me for that matter. But know this baby girl. I'm not going anywhere. I'm staying right here. The moment I found out about you a sought you out and found you."

People were passing by the car and backing their cars out of the parking lot. The radio clock read a quarter past twelve pm. At this moment nothing around us mattered. It was just her and I.

"I had a father once," I said.

"Really?" Said Grace.

"Yes," I said.

"But he abandoned me. Cast me out like I was nothing. He has nothing to do with me now." I said.

"I think I know how the rest of the story goes." Said Grace while mildly chuckling.

This made me smile.

"The fact is, he did that. But I will never ever do that to you." I said while looking over at her making eye contact with me.

The shades of blue in her eyes reminded me of her mother's eyes. They were as blue as a cloudless sky.

"I believe you." Said Grace.

I stretched my wings that were tucked in my jeans. It was slightly uncomfortable. The retraction process involving an angel's wings was pretty complex. You had to hold your breath and concentrate on bending your shoulder blades inwards. It was the only way to walk amongst mortals. Like I've been saying being caught out in the open by one of my brothers or by Dad himself, since he is always watching would be dire. Grace picked up on me being uncomfortable. She was pretty observant.

"Your wings hurt don't they?" She asked.

"Slightly, yes," I replied.

"Can I ask you a question?" She said.
"I don't see why not," I said.
Another deep sigh was let out by her.
"Mom won't let me, but I think I'm ready."
"Ready for what?" I replied to Grace.
"I think I'm ready to learn how to fly." She said.

I leaned over the steering wheel watching the people coming in and out of the store, then looked back over at Grace who was carefully studying my every move.

"Do you know the golden rule?" I asked.
"Yes. Mom told me. Don't ever get caught by a mortal in your angelic form."
"Precisely. Don't ever let someone see your wings. Otherwise, you could shift." I said.
"Shift?" Asked Grace.
"Yes. Shifting is when an immortal shifts into a mortal and turns to ash and dies." I said.

Honesty at this point was the best policy. There was no beating around the bush with her. I had to tell her like it was. She concentrated hard on her next question before asking.

"So. Last night is that what was starting to happen to you?" Asked Grace.

"Yes. That's exactly what was happening. But the caffeine balanced me out and you saved me and this vessel. Speaking of which I could use some caffeine right about now." I said.

"So will you teach me how to fly?" She asked while smiling at me.

I knew Rachel would eventually have to let her take to her wings and fly. Who better to teach her how than her own father.

"Yes, I will teach you." I said.
"Yay!" She said with excitement and leaned in to hug me.

We embraced for several seconds before letting go. It was a nice feeling. I felt as if a piece of me had been restored.

"But first we got to take care of business," I said.

"What's that?" She said as she pulled away from hugging me.

"We have to go bra shopping," I said while chuckling.

"Yes. Yes we do." She said as we both laughed.

I killed the ignition to the car and pulled the keys out of the ignition and slipped them into my right pocket.

"Come on let's go inside," I said.

"Okay." Said Grace as she stepped out of the car and shut the door.

Morningstar Chapter 32

"See that was painless." Said Grace.

I carried the bags of clothes and bras to the car for her. She pressed the trunk button which opened up the back hatch slowly. It was automated.

"Painless, yes. That's not the issue." I said while getting into the driver's seat.

Grace got into the passenger seat and closed the door and started to put her seatbelt on.

"Then what is the issue?" Asked Grace.

I started the ignition. It was hot. Kansas was known for its hot summers. I turned on the a/c and cracked the windows to get some of the heat out for Grace.

"The issue is you're growing up," I said.

"So." Said Grace.

"I've missed so much. It's just time I can't get back." I said to Grace.

She put on her newly acquired pink sunglasses she had just bought from inside the store before responding.

"Then make time now." She said while looking at her reflection in the visor mirror on the passenger side.

It dawned on me that she was wise beyond her years. She was in the now, not the past, not the future, but the moments of today. We were making memories.

"You're right. Let's go have some fun." I said while adjusting the rearview mirror.

I also bought some sunglasses. Black framed with dark lenses. I was putting them on and looking at how they looked in the rearview mirror.

"What do you have in mind, Lu?" She asked while studying me admiring my new sunglasses.

The air in the car was finally blowing cold air. I rolled up the windows and put the car in reverse.

"I was thinking we go get some ice cream for us and Mom. What do you think about that?" I asked Grace.

"Mmm Ice cream sounds really good." Said Grace.

Grace's cell phone started to vibrate. Repeatedly over and over. It was laying in the center console of the Traverse. It vibrated various quarters and pennies that lay about in the center console.

"It's probably Mom." She said.

We pulled out of the parking lot back onto the way we had come passed the other storefronts towards the main stripe of the town. The town of Haven wasn't that big. But it also, wasn't that little either. The population was just a tad over eight hundred people. I let out a smile. I was truly enjoying life for once.

"Tell her I said hello," I said to Grace while concentrating on driving.

"I missed it." Said Grace.

"Call her back. She what flavor of ice cream she wants." I said.

"Lu." Said Grace.

I looked over at her.

"What is it?" I said feeling the weight of her saying my name in that manner.

"It wasn't Mom." Said Grace.

"Oh? Who was it then?" I asked.

"I have five missed calls all from the home nurse, and one from Mom thirty minutes ago while we were in the store." Said Grace now in a slight panic.

She quickly dialed back the home nurse and put it on speaker. It rang for what seemed like forever. Then it went straight to voicemail.

"Call Mom." I said now picking up speed through the main strip of town.

Grace was beginning to panic. Her breathing started to change followed by her hands trembling. She quickly hung up the phone call to the voicemail of the home nurse and dialed Rachel. It rang. It rang again. And again.

"She's not picking up!" She yelled.

I pushed my foot on the accelerator. I watched as the needle on the speedometer climbed from the speed limit of twenty-five to nearly fifty miles per hour. I was headed back to the house. Something didn't feel quite right. Her phone made a noise as if she had just gotten some notification.

"Lu!" Said Grace.

"What is it!" I snapped.

"There's a voicemail from Mom." Said Grace.

I looked over at Grace briefly then back at the road. We still had a bit of a way to go before we would make it back to the house.

"Play it. Put it on speaker." I said.

The tone of the voicemail was muffled at first. It sounded like that crying and sniffling. All of the sudden her voice came through the voicemail.

"Honey, it's me, Mom. You guys need to come home now. I need Lu to come home now." Said Rachel in the voicemail.

Then another voice came through the phone. It made me instantly angry.

"And make sure he brings me my money, you stupid bitch." Said Josh.

The next thing that could be heard is some more sobbing from Rachel. Then the voicemail ended.

"Lu." Said Grace.

"I know. Hold on." I said while turning around a sharp left turn, up the road to the house.

We were nearly there with the speed that we were going.

"What are you going to do to Josh?" Asked Grace.

She asked me again what I was going to do.

I didn't respond. I was hyper-fixated on one thing. I was going to kill him.

Morningstar Chapter 33

We pulled into the driveway of the house nearly hitting the mailbox that had Rachel's and Grace's handprints on it. Gravel kicked up behind the Traverse with the speed I was going. The time on the radio read nearly three fifty pm. There was a motorcycle in the driveway, as well as the home nurse's vehicle.

"That's Josh's motorcycle!" Shouted Grace.

I pulled into the driveway going nearly fifty miles per hour.

"Stay here," I said to Grace while shifting the car into park.

"But–". Said Grace before I could slam the door closed.

"Grace No. You don't need to see what happens next." I said while slamming the car door closed.

I couldn't focus on that. I needed to keep Grace safe and see what Josh was doing with Rachel. He had to have known we pulled up, especially with the way I had pulled up the driveway.

"Josh!" I screamed out.

A figure could be seen moving from the window looking in, and then disappearing from out of view. I marched up the steps of the house and kicked the front door in. Pieces of the door flew inward onto the floor, scattering about in the hallway inside.

Blood filled my vision. A pool of it was on the floor in front of me as I stepped inside. Josh had murdered the home health nurse. Her corpse lay there helplessly inside the kitchen. She had been shot repeatedly.

"Lucifer!" Cried out Rachel from down the hallway.

The door where her voice was coming from was left open. It was Rachel's room from down the inner hallway. Josh was holding her from behind with a gun pointed at her head.

"Please Lu, Help–." Said Rachel before being cut off by Josh.

"Shut it you stupid bitch. Now that you're here. You can give me my money right now." Demanded Josh.

I was in the hallway about twenty-five feet from Josh and Rachel.

Josh's face was still burnt from the night before when I had thrown coffee on him.

"Or what?" I said while snarling.

I could feel the rage coursing through my body.

"Or I blow her bald head to pieces." He shouted from behind Rachel.

"Babe," I said.

"Yeah?" She said squirming while being held onto by Josh.

"Everything's going to be okay," I said while looking her in the eyes.

She nodded, as a single tear came out of her right eye and rolled down her cheek.

Josh aimed at the back of her head and took a step back.

"Time's up!" Yelled Josh.

I smiled and my eyes rolled into the back of my head. I was going to destroy him. Josh was getting ready to pull the trigger. That's when I knew I needed to react fast. In this case, I had a trick up my sleeve. I snapped my fingers and time stood still. Everything and everybody in the close area was now frozen in time. Everybody was unable to comprehend what was going on, and unable to even know that time itself was frozen still. I ripped off my shirt and spread my wings down the hallway. Barrel rolling all the way to Rachel and Josh. Even though she was frozen I could see the fear in her eyes. I gently grabbed her by the shoulders and moved her slightly to the side of the room away from Josh. Josh's finger was on the trigger, which was slightly squeezed.

"I told you I'd make you suffer," I said to him.

He was frozen, but I took this to my advantage. I took his arm that was holding the gun and manipulated his arm to where the gun was now facing his left kneecap. I wanted to end it right there. But I wasn't finished with him. I held up my hand, piercing my gaze into his eyes, and snapped my fingers again. Everything came rushing back. Nothing was frozen any longer. Josh pulled the trigger completely, with the gun facing his knee. The ringing from the gunshot was louder than the screams of pain he let out. Blood went flying everywhere.

"Ah, fuck!" Screamed Josh as he collapsed to the floor.

His knee was done for. He instantly started whimpering.

"Look at me," I said as I stood over him.

He opened his eyes looking up at me, and then away concentrating all his focus on his kneecap he had just obliterated.

"You won't look at me then I'll take your sight away!" I shouted.

I forced his eyes open with my fingers and pressed my thumbs into his eye sockets. I pushed until both of my thumbs were all the way in his eye sockets.

He let out an excruciating yell. Blood was now trickling down his face and around where his eyes once were. He screamed. I was done with this guy terrorizing my girls. No more would he breathe in the mortal world. I leaned his head back by his chin, exposing his Adam's apple and in one swift motion I slammed my fist down on his windpipe crushing it instantly. He was gone. In a matter of seconds, his body convulsed and stopped twitching altogether.

"Mom!" Screamed Grace who had made her way into the house.

I still had my fist drawn back waiting for him to move again. My fist hovered above the bloody leftovers of Josh.

"Lucifer, that's enough. He's gone." Said Rachel.

I made eye contact with her and got up off my knees and took a breath in. The rage was still coursing through my body. I needed to come back to terms with reality in this realm. My girls were safe and Josh was no more. That's what I needed to focus on.

Now I had a mess to clean up.

Morningstar Chapter 34

"You killed him." Said Grace.

I took a deep breath and exhaled lowering my fist that was still raised above the remnants of Josh. Blood covered the floor in various areas. When I hit him with my fist in his windpipe, I hit him with the same force I used against Michael. Blood dripped from my fist onto the ground.

"I did. It needed to be done." I said.

I was gaining my sense of control back. I was finding my center. I was calming down.

"Grace hunny, I need you to try and understand." Said Rachel while comforting Grace.

"It's not that Mom. I'm just happy it's finally over. I'm happy he got what he deserved." Said Grace.

I snapped back to the reality of things altogether. The girls were my center. I could hear their conversation off in the corner of the room.

"What do we do now Lu?" Asked Rachel in a concerned tone.

My eyes rolled back to normal. No longer were they in the back of my head.

They only did that whenever I was beyond mad and past self-control. I turned around to face the girls, which my back was to.

"We need to get rid of the bodies. Preferably around sundown. That way none of the nearby neighbors can see what's going on. We also hope that the law wasn't called whenever he killed the nurse and when he fired the shot into his kneecap." I said.

I tried to wrap my head around what to do next other than what I had just told them.

"Honestly I'm just glad you are okay Rachel. When I heard the voicemail my heart sank." I said.

"Mine too Mom. I think we were both panicking." Said Grace.

"I've never seen so much blood before." Said Grace.

The color in her face was starting to change to that of a pale white. You could tell she wasn't feeling good.

"I think I'm going to be sick." She said before puking on the floor near her mother.

She was dry heaving at this point. I had to get them out of the room and clean up the mess I had created. Blood was starting to ooze around what was left of Josh.

"You girls go into the other room and keep a lookout for anybody that might be coming this way into the driveway. I'll get this cleaned up." I said.

"What are you going to do with–" Said Rachel.

"I'll said I'll handle it, dear, so let me handle it," I said.

At this point, Grace had stopped dry heaving. She looked at me as Rachel gently took her out of the room. Her eyes spoke words in that instant.

She didn't have to say anything. She was thankful that I had taken care of Josh and kept Rachel safe.

"Rachel," I said while she was almost out of the room, standing in the doorway with grace.

Rachel looked back at me while still holding Grace by the shoulders. Grace didn't turn around, instead, she continued to stare down the hallway. She acknowledged me, waiting for whatever I had to say.

"I love you," I said as my wings fluttered when I moved my shoulders.

"I love you too Lu." Said Rachel.

"Do you have any trash bags?" I asked.

She smirked for a split second before responding.

"Everything you should need is in the shed, outside. Cover up your wings and go outside and get the heavy-duty black bags, and whatever, tools you might need." Said Rachel.

She was still holding Grace as they took a step forward down the hallway further away from me.

"Also you have this mess in here to clean up as well." Said Rachel.

She was referring to the home nurse. I was surprised how well she was actually handling all of this. But she and I have had our issues in the past. Between my late-night drinking and near-death experience as of recent, things like that change a person. They make them numb. To the point they don't feel situations like others do anymore. I knew this at least, we still loved each other and that's all that mattered in the end.

"I'll handle it, babe." I said.

"I know you will." Said Rachel as she stepped out down the hallway with Grace and into Grace's bedroom.tg6tttttttttt

I let out a deep sigh while staring down at what was left of Josh.

"May you burn in hell you piece of shit," I said.

I started to walk down the hallway. Looking at the various family photos of Rachel and Grace. It made me smile to see them so happy. I wanted to be a part of that. But I questioned even my own existence. Was I even allowed to be happy? Was I just a mistake? After all, I was the one that tempted Dad's creation in the Garden. I needed some air. I needed to clear my head. I stepped carefully over the home nurse's body that was on the floor by the front door. Pieces of the door that I had kicked in had riddled the top of her body like sawdust and wood chips on a carpenter. I leaned down over her body.

"I'm sorry. May you rest in peace." I said.

I realized what would be happening next. The small amount of wind that was coming into the house through the broken-down front door, stopped altogether. It's as if time itself was standing still. Then

I felt it. The shadow of something standing at the front door was watching me. I knew who it was. I stood to my feet gazing at the entrance of the house.

"Hello, Michael," I said.

His eyes stayed on me not moving in the slightest. A yellow shimmer in his eyes caught my attention. Then he sighed.

"You and I need to talk. Let's go." Said Michael.

Morningstar Chapter 35

Michael and I had made our way out to the shed in the backyard. Birds that were in the sky were frozen. Nothing moving, and not a sound was being made with nearby traffic on the other side of the woods next to the house. Even the clouds that were over our heads weren't moving. Not even a hint of wind was around us. He had frozen everything around us. You see, you have to understand something about my brother. One of his duties as part of Dad's army was to make sure souls ascended to Heaven. In this case, he was here to ascend the home nurse, that Josh brutally killed to get to Rachel.

"I don't even know where to start with you." Said Michael.

"I'm not sure what you want me to say to that brother," I said.

He pointed his finger into my face and his wings went up, as if they were on alert. He made two steps towards me.

"Don't." He said in a stern tone.

"Don't what?" I responded.

"Don't call me a brother. You're no brother of mine." Said Michael.

I kicked at the ground while placing my hands on my hips and raising my wings. They almost equally matched his with height and wingspan. The only difference is his were white, and mine were black.

"So what, are we doing this again or what?" I said while cracking my neck from side to side.

"No." Responded Michael.

"Dad sent me." He said.

I chuckled.

"Another test I presume?" I said while clenching my fists, waiting for his next move.

"Not this time." He said.

"Then what are you doing here?" I asked.

He took another step towards me, throwing his hands up in the air and letting them land back at his side.

"I should ask you the same thing." He said.

It was apparent that he didn't know all the details of what had taken place.

Only what he was told.

I patted him on the chest, twice.

"Wouldn't you like to know." I said.

His eyes glimmered yellow into my eyes.

"Don't touch me." Said Michael in a stern tone.

I rolled my eyes. I was annoyed.

"Got it. Don't touch. Calm down there, soldier." I said while quietly chuckling.

One of the shed doors was open while the other remained closed. It wasn't much to look at. Most of the floorboards from what I could tell were rotted through or falling inwards. Honestly, it was a piece of shit, but it's where the tools and trash bags were.

"I have a soul to ascend. That's all I know." Said Michael.

This was good. That means he didn't know about the girls being in Grace's bedroom. Nor did he know of what I did to Josh in the back bedroom. As far as he was concerned he was here to collect a soul and leave.

"My question is why are you here?" He asked while peering into my eyes.

I thought about my response briefly, before responding. It wasn't a question that I had to answer. Nor was I about to tell him anything about Grace or Rachel being in the bedroom. It wasn't his place to know. If Dad wanted him to know, he would have told him. The Kansas sunset was beautiful to look at briefly. It was the only thing that continued to move slightly as we stood outside. His abilities of freezing time only went so far. Everything within close proximity couldn't move. I knew the girls were a part of this as well. They wouldn't come storming out of the bedroom. Everything was okay for now, depending on my response.

"I'm on my way, to Eden," I said.

Michael's eyes got big and curious.

"Eden?" He said.

"Yes, you heard me correctly. Dad's orders." I said.

He had a look on his face of disbelief.

"A little far away from Eden don't you think?" He said.

"Running the clock down a little on ascending a soul, don't you think?" I said in snark comeback.

He took a step back. Then another.

"You're right. For once." He said as he started to walk away from the shed.

His back was now turned to me. I studied his wings for several seconds admiring the beauty of them.

"I can feel your eyes on me Lucifer." He said as he stopped walking while leaning his head over his shoulder, back in my direction.

"I just–," I said before being interrupted.

"You miss it, don't you? What's it like brother?" He said as he turned back around to face me.

"What's what like?" I said.

"Not being wanted. Not being loved. Being in the position you're in, and being cursed to walk the Earth for all eternity." He said.

This set me off. Rage started to course through my veins. I could feel anger clouding my judgment. I had to be careful with my next move. I knew this much at least. I took a deep breath in and exhaled. I was trying this new thing called self-control.

"There he is." Said Michael.

"Go do your job, Daddy's boy," I said as I grabbed the trash bags from the shed.

"This isn't over between us." Said Michael.

"As it always isn't," I said.

He made his way back to the front of the house. Back into the entryway of the door, I had kicked in just an hour ago or so. He made his way into the house and leaned down by the nurse.

He began to whisper a prayer. It was loud enough that I could hear.

"Father. Ascend this soul into your loving arms. May I as a servant and creation of you carry on this soul as we ascend together. Amen." Said Michael.

He raised his hands into the air above her body and a small spherical blue ball came up out of her chest. He cupped it into his hands. The blue light illuminated his hands. It was her soul. It was his duty to ascend pure hearts into Heaven. As for Josh, it wasn't his concern. He wouldn't be ascending.. Michael's eyes were still closed, he was in a trance. I wasn't going to interfere. I needed him gone, so I could get back to my girls and clean up the rest of my mess.

He stood to his feet and started to walk back out the front door. I got out of his way. Stepping back and even extending my hand outwards in a kind gesture as if signifying, you first. As he walked by he carefully continued to cup his hands together. The blue light, her essence, her soul, was pure enough to ascend. He walked down the steps of the concrete porch steps onto the grass. He leaned his head up to sky, the clouds started to move overhead slowly. Birds wings begun to move slowly. Everything was in slow motion but it was quickly starting to speed back up, and become unfrozen.

"I'll be seeing you around Lucifer." Said Michael.

Then just like that, he ascended up in the air, still cupping his hands together holding her soul. Then within a blink of the eye he had launched himself with his wings in one swift motion above the clouds and out of view. He was gone. Everything had returned to normal. No time had passed by hardly at all. I got myself inside because I was still shirtless and my wings were exposed to the far off neighboring house.

Not a car was in sight, regardless I had to be careful. I didn't want to expose myself in angelic form to any mortals. So many things were left unanswered. My daughter, her wings. My soul purpose was to try and spend as much time as possible with both Rachel and Grace. They were my everything at this point. But I had things I needed to do. I needed to teach Grace how to fly. I needed to go to Eden. I needed to partake of the fruit from the tree. Then what? What would happen to me then? Would I shift and die. Would I perish and be a lost soul that wouldn't ascend?

The light was beginning to fade through the windows of the house. Soon it would be dark and I and dark were friends. I could get rid of Josh and dispose of the nurse's body properly.

"Everything okay?" Said Rachel on the otherside of Grace's bedroom door.

And then in that moment, I told her the a lie.

"Everything's fine babe. Everything's fine." I said while staring at the wall in the entrance of the house.

She didn't need to know about Michael. As far as she was concerned I had only been gone outside for a minute or two.

"Everything's fine just got to finish up, out here," I said as I opened up a large black trash bag, I had got from the shed.

Morningstar Chapter 36

The midnight Kansas moon was high in the sky. The motorcycle was the last thing I needed to get rid of. A nearby lake about two miles to the north of the house made it easy to get rid of the car. I parked the nurse's vehicle by the lake boat dock and started to return to the house. Her soul was taken care of. She had ascended with Michael. I put the gun in the trunk of the car. The same gun that Josh had used against the nurse. Along with her body neatly wrapped in trash bags. Those trash bags didn't need to have a reference point back to the girls. So I got rid of the entire box and threw what remained in a small trash can along the walking path of the lake. I didn't need to worry about fingerprints. Angels, even the fallen had no fingerprints. The most important thing was that I could clean up this mess the best I could. There was no point in getting the law involved. It would just create more problems for the girls.

As for Josh's body, I laid him out about a quarter of a mile away from the parked nurse's car. I tucked a trash bag into his right pocket of his jeans that was riddled with his fingerprints. If you hadn't caught on yet, I was framing Josh. His fingerprints were all over the gun that was in the trunk. They were all over the trash bag that the nurse was wrapped in within the trunk as well. The trash bag in his pocket was there for looks, mostly for authorities. I needed to make it appear that he did it of his own free will.

A sign caught my attention as I was leaving the lake where the road split to the right and to the left. It read, "Haven Lake, no dumping no admission after dark." I chuckled slightly.

"Looks like I'm a rule breaker." I thought as I continued to walk back to the house.

The roadside was full of litter. Various cups and beer bottles were thrown out by teenagers and drivers who didn't care about littering. Thick tree lines were on the left side and right side of the road. Beyond the tree lines that were on the side of the road, were fields. Fields full of various crops and cattle. If I listened closely I could hear the cows far out in the fields that surrounded me as I continued to walk closer back to Rachel and Grace's house. There wasn't a residential house for another mile or so. I looked up at the sky and studied the moon. Its features remained intact. Not a thing about it had changed throughout my banishment here, other than a few impact craters, that had happened over the centuries. I watched as a commercial plane flew overhead with its red light, lighting up every few seconds high up in the sky. It made me long to fly as well. But I couldn't. Not now. Now all that mattered was getting rid of the rest of the mess back at the house.

I had passed my first house on the right side of the road. I knew I was getting close. I wasn't worried about the condition of Josh either. The coyotes and buzzards would make quick work of his body. Whatever was left by the time his body was reported in the morning would be enough to rule it out as what looked like a murder-suicide. Although I did wonder what they would think of his crushed windpipe. None of that honestly mattered, however. The road to walk up to the house was coming up. I walked up the path of the driveway, passed the mailbox of Rachel and Grace, and saw Grace standing on the front porch with a broom in hand. Rachel was sitting in a chair on the porch. Grace was sweeping the various broken pieces of wood from the front door into a pile.

I smiled and waved at them as I walked up the gravel driveway. Rachel waved back at me. I could hear them having a conversation but I wasn't close enough to hear exactly what was being said. I turned on my angelic senses. As weird as that sounds it works. Having heightened abilities to hear conversations was one of many things that I could do.

"Honey just keep sweeping it up in a pile and Lu will take care of the bag for us." Said Rachel.

"Okay, Mom." Said Grace.

I was now within listening and talking distance from the front porch. The small porchlight illuminated a portion of the porch and Rachel remained in the dark. Not a portion of the porchlight touched her. The faint glow of a cigarette in her mouth illuminated the darkness.

"Are you– are you smoking?" I asked.

Rachel took another hit off of the cigarette before responding and exhaling the smoke into the air.

"Oh, it's just one. I'm already dying at this point so what does it matter!" She snapped.

"I'm sorry I just–," I said before being cut off.

Rachel stood to her feet and threw the cigarette on the concrete porch and put it out with her foot.

"We're all just a little stressed Lu. That was a lot to take in." Said Rachel.

I grabbed the dustpan that was near Grace's feet. She continued to sweep the woodchips into a pile. Her hands were shaking as she swept the remaining bits into a pile. I held the dustpan still for her as she quickly realized what I was doing. She swept the pile into the dustpan and I threw away what had remained into the trash bag.

I took the trash bag and sat it down by the motorcycle.

"Look I know you girls have both just been through so much. And I'm to blame for that. I just want you two to be safe and have the best possible life. I would lay down my life for you two. My perspective on life over the last few days has changed completely. I love you two, with every breath that runs through me." I said as I got on the motorcycle.

"Where are you going?" Asked Grace.

"I got to get rid of the motorcycle," I said.

Rachel was thinking. She was always thinking.

"You get rid of that motorcycle and come back to us. We got a door to replace" Said Rachel.

"We love you too." Said Grace.

It was at this moment that I realized something. I was wanted. I was loved and on top of everything I was needed.

I rolled out the motorcycle with my feet, pushing it backward and down the driveway. Not with it started of course. I didn't want to alarm any nearby neighbors with the motor started. I knew exactly where Josh's body was at the lake and that was where I'd be taking the motorcycle.

MorningStar Chapter 37

"Did you take care of it?" Asked Rachel.

I was back at the house. The deed was done. All was as if it had never happened besides the front door.

"I took care of it," I said to Rachel.

"Good. That's good. Grace is asleep. Everything–Everything is good." She said.

Rachel was weak. I could see it in her as she tried to look like she was holding it together.

"Are you okay?" I asked while extending my arm out to grab her from falling.

It was apparent that the answer was no. I didn't know how many more moons and suns I could share with her, but I wanted them to last for eternity.

"The cancer is winning Lucifer. I don't have much longer." She said.

"What can I do for you, my love?" I said.

We had moved into the living room area, to make her more comfortable. I carefully set her down on the couch as she laid back resting her head on some throw pillows that were on there. She looked up at me with her beautiful eyes and gently touched the side of my face with her brittle cold hand.

"I need you to end it." Said Rachel.

"I want all the pain to stop. I want to just be able to let go and know that Grace is going to be okay. You can take care of this for me, right? You'll do that for me, won't you?" She asked.

I stumbled on the wording of her request. Was she asking me to end her suffering? How could I possibly even muster up the strength to do such a task?

"Rachel. I can't end your pain. I'm sorry I've been a part of that pain as well in the past. But I can't physically do what you are requesting." I said as calmly as I could.

"And the other thing?" She said as a single tear came down of her face and rolled down her cheek.

"The other thing?" I responded.

She smiled.

"You never were good at listening Lu. The other thing is that you'll make sure Grace is okay, right?" She said as her eyes began to get heavy.

Her shallow breathing worried me. She was taking multiple breaths that sounded like she was having difficulty inhaling. I grabbed her hand as she lay on the couch and held onto it firmly cupping my other hand around it.

"I promise I will take care of her until I draw my last breath," I said.

"Lu." She said faintly.

Her color was changing and her chest was slowing down in its rising with each breath that she took.

"Yes, my moon?" I said.

"Don't be sad. But I think I have to go now." Said Rachel almost as if she was whispering.

"Go? Go where? You're not leaving me, babe." I said sternly.

A smile formed on her face as she stared up at the ceiling. She was in awe.

"It's so beautiful Lu. It's unbelievably magnificent." She said as she closed her eyes.

"No-No-No! No!" I said as I cradled her in my arms.

"I'll love— I'll love you forever Lucifer." She said as her smile faded to that of a still blank expression.

That was it. She was gone. Her body just couldn't take it anymore. She had been through too much for too long. I screamed out.

"Rachel! Come on babe! Come on baby! Come back to me!" I said slightly shaking her.

Her arms collapsed to her sides, hanging off of the couch.

"No-No-Nooooooo!" I shouted, with my wings ripping through the shirt I had on and spreading out as far as they could.

I leaned my forehead against Rachel's and started to weep. Tears were falling off my face onto her face. Her face was expressionless. There was nothing there. Not anymore. My beautiful baby was gone. I held onto her body for what felt like minutes. I cradled her, rocking her back in forth in my lap. My wings were still spread out to their maximum length. I was a wreck.

That's when it happened.

"Lu?" Said Grace from down the hallway, where her room was.

"Don't come in here!" I said.

It was already too late. She had rounded the corner and was standing in the entryway of the living room. She took in everything. Me, Rachel, all of it.

"Mom?" She said faintly.

"Mommy?" She said again in a more concerned tone.

She had brushed past my wings and leaned down by her mother's head.

"Oh no, Mom. No!" She screamed.

It was painful to watch and experience. Grace had fallen into the kneeling position by her mother's head and gently rubbed it in a slow fashion. Tears were forming in her eyes.

"Bring her back Lu." She said as she cleared the tears from her eyes looking up at me.

"I can't. I can't do tha–." I said as I was pushed back on my chest with her fists.

"Bring my mom back now!" She demanded in a sharp tone while hitting her small fist against my chest.

Her wings shuffled under her shirt. I saw as her shoulders began to rise. With one quick motion, a wing ripped out from underneath her shirt and out and about, quickly followed by the other one. She was in pain as well. Probably way more than I was. She stretched out her wings in such a fashion that I watched as they grew twice the size they had normally appeared to be within seconds.

"My beautiful mother! She's– She's–." She said choking up on her words.

"She's gone. I'm so sorry honey. I'm so sorry." I said.

Grace was a complete wreck. All I could do was extend my arms out as we hugged and cried together.

Time started to slow. It slowed all the way down. It was Michael. He was coming to collect a soul and ascend.

MorningStar Chapter 38

I noticed something was different this time. Grace wasn't being affected by it. In fact, she was still sobbing in my arms. She wasn't frozen as I thought she was earlier when Michael came to ascend the home health nurse's soul.

"Grace. I need you to get behind me." I said.

"What?" Grace replied.

"There's no time to explain I need you to listen to me and get behind me," I said while standing up, and keeping an eye on the front door.

"What's happening?" Asked Grace.

She was scared, hurt, and confused all at once.

"It's your uncle, Michael. He's here." I said.

She got to her feet and stood behind me in the living room area. There wasn't much room. Especially on account of our wingspans. Mine were charcoal colored, Grace's was snow white. Within seconds of our conversation, a gushing of wind could be heard outside. Michael had just landed. I heard as he hit the ground. A gush of air could be felt brisking by us.

"What does he want?" Asked Grace.

"Don't say anything," I said.

Through the entryway of the busted-up doorframe, Michael had appeared. Staring at the lifeless body of Rachel, with his hands folded as if he was in prayer.

"Care to explain?" He said.

He knelt by her body. I choked on my words. I knew what he was doing.

"Don't touch her!" Shouted Grace from back behind me.

She had pushed her way from behind me to confront Michael.

Michael was a giant compared to Grace.

"And whom might you be?" Demanded Michael.

"I'm Grace, and I'm telling you not to touch my damn mother!" She snapped.

Michael's head gave it away. He instantly looked away from Rachel's corpse and straight into Grace's eyes and stood to his feet.

"You? Your mom? Wait a second." He said studying Grace's wings.

"That's enough Michael," I said staring through him.

If he thought for one second I was going to put up with his shit, he was in for a rude awakening.

"Little one what is your rank? Whom do you serve?" He demanded, asking one question after the other.

She didn't respond. I pulled her back to the side of me, to keep her at bay from my brother. He didn't need to know anything more than what he had already found out.

Michael waited for several seconds before wiping that look off his face. You know the look, the one where you're waiting for an answer from someone.

"No matter. I'll find out, as I always do. " He said.

He had put his focus back on Rachel. His right hand hovered above her face as he chanted something in angelic dialect.

"What are you– doing to her." Asked Grace.

She had pushed her hair out of her face and wiped a few tears away.

"Your mom is going with me." Said Michael.

"To where?" Asked Grace.

"Heaven," replied Michael.

A blue aura shot up from Rachel's chest It floated there for several seconds before rising higher up into the air. A small spherical orb was in Michael's hands. All was silent. Grace didn't interfere. Nor did I. We watched, together. I knew that her soul would soon ascend with Michael.

I thought of the memories we had shared. The coffee house all those years ago. The years of tormenting each other. The laughter and even the tears.

I comforted Grace. I gently laid my hand on her shoulder.

"It's going to be okay," I whispered to her.

I thought of all the time I wasted drinking in random bars when I could have just been there for her. For the both of them. Drinking had such a hold on me, that I didn't even realize it at the time.

Michael stood up from her body. He took a few steps away from us, before turning back around.

"I don't know what this is. But if it's what I think it is, Father won't be pleased." Said Michael.

He then walked out of the house onto the front lawn, we could see him through the window, even though it was dark outside. He then flapped his wings once and hovered off of the ground. A noise that can only be described as majestic was made, every time he flapped his wings. A cool breeze had set into the house. Grace and I continued to watch him through the living room window. Then just like that, he was gone. He flew far into the sky. Straight up into the air he launched himself. The noises of his wings flapping became quieter until no noise could be heard.

Tears were still rolling off of the face of Grace. She was sniffling. I wanted nothing more than to help stop the pain she was feeling and experiencing.

"Grace I'm so sorry. I'm sorry you're having to go through any of this." I said.

Could you imagine, a nine-year-old girl, who is half angel, half human with a mother dying from cancer, and no other living family members to comfort her? Other than her father that's been out of the picture until about a week ago?

"What do we do now?" Said Grace in a faint voice.

She had hugged me tightly around my waist, looking up to me in the process. She was completely lost. My pain was nowhere compared to hers. She had just lost her best friend, her rock, the one true person that was always there for her.

"We make arrangements my dear," I said.

Morningstar Chapter 39

Nobody came but Grace, myself, and the funeral home director. Sun shined through the stained glass windows of the funeral home. It was beyond bright. Luckily for me, I brought my sunglasses. It hid my watery eyes. Grace had found a black dress to wear. I used the money we still had to buy a decent suit and tie and buy a decent funeral service for Rachel. A picture of Rachel that Grace had found was displayed by her urn. God I loved that smile in that photo. It stuck out to me, more than anything. It was indeed her best quality. I realized at this point I couldn't see that beautiful smile one last time. My darling was gone. Tears started to roll down my face. I tried my best to keep it together for Grace's sake.

We decided to cremate instead of bury, on account of her last wishes.

A video file was saved on her computer with a document signed by an attorney. The video declared my rights as a caretaker to Grace. I wasn't technically a person: no birth certificate, no traceable documentation of any kind. I knew DHS and Child Protective Services would soon be by, upon knowing of Rachel's death. But I had that handled. I wasn't worried in the slightest.

In the video, she also said:

"You'll think I'm crazy but I'm leaving the house to you Lucifer."

I could see her hooked up and receiving some kind of medicine. Most likely painkillers. This was recorded moments before the Nurse was killed on account of the timestamp on the video. We still hadn't received a phone call from her multiple times yet.

"I know you can be persuasive. So I'm not worried about the situation with you and Grace. I know you'll do right by her. I'm just so pleased that you are here, with us. I don't know how much more time I have, but I want every moment to be shared with you two." Said Rachel in the video.

We had met with the attorney yesterday to square away the details. A little persuasion went a long way. I had convinced the lawyer that I had proper documentation, and I smoothed it over with some deep eye contact. It of course worked like a charm. I had also taken the opportunity to put up a temporary front door. We had spent the night before last crying and mostly laughing about the good times. It gave me an opportunity to open up to Grace about the times Rachel and I had spent together. Grace reached out to hold my hand and grasped it tightly as tears poured down her face.

"Is there anything the family would like to say on behalf of Rachel?" Said the Funeral director at the podium.

We were the only two there besides the assistant funeral director, who was standing by the entryway of the funeral home. It was set up much like a small church. Light poured in from opposite directions on the left and right side of the church pews.

I stood to my feet, I felt the overwhelming urge to say something on behalf of my beloved Rachel. But Grace had also stood up. She looked at me as I looked over at her. She stepped out of that pew and walked down the aisle. Each step she took felt as if she was shedding some kind of weight from her heart. She took a breath before saying anything into the microphone.

"To my dearest mother. I know that cancer ultimately destroyed you in the end, but what it didn't destroy was our love for one another. You raised me from this small thing, into who I am today." Said Grace.

"I remember all the oldies music, cruising down the street with the wind blowing in our hair. I remember all the times you told me that I was unique and loved in a multitude of different ways." She said holding back tears.

"I also remember you saying I was special. That there was a reason for my existence. I still believe that. I'll hold onto that. Until one day we meet again." Said Grace.

At this point, she had grabbed the podium as small tears rolled down her cheeks and off of her chin, one by one.

***

"I LOVE YOU FOREVER and ever. Good–. Goodbye, Mother." Said Grace as she came out from behind the podium and walked back to her seat by me.

The funeral director made his way back to the stage area and began to talk into the microphone.

"At this time the family has prepared a short slide show with photos of their loved one and videos of Rachel Fairborn." Said the funeral director as a projector screen lowered down to the right of the podium.

The slide show started. There were smiles, there was laughter, and most of all there were tears shared between Grace and me, during those few minutes of the slide show. My wings were restless. I needed to break free and go fly for a while. Grace looked over at me. I could feel her eyes on me.

"Lu." Said Grace.

"Yes, What is it, hun?" I asked.

"I'm ready." Said Grace as she stood to her feet.

"Ready for what?" I asked.

She adjusted her shoulders back and forth and looked up towards the ceiling, she balled up her fists.

"For you to teach me how to fly." She said as plainly as she could.

I nodded and stood to my feet.

"Let's go then," I said.

"Where are we going?" Asked Grace.

"I'm going to teach you how to fly," I said.

Morningstar Chapter 40

We had traveled in the Traverse for quite some time outside of city limits. The air passed by us and made my wings flutter. The sun was still shining brightly in the sky, although it was quickly on its descent out of view within the next few hours.

"Why do we have to go all this way?" Asked Grace.

I was gripping the steering wheel enjoying a clover cigar I had bought earlier. I was careful to ensure the smoke didn't fill up the vehicle's cab. I carefully blew my smoke out the driver's side window that I had down. The wind felt nice blowing against my face. Grace also had her window down. Her hair on her head blew all over in the wind. She was enjoying the moment, as was I.

"Because nobody can see us in our angelic form," I said.

"I don't get it?" Said Grace.

"No mortal shall see us in our angelic form. It's a precaution that you must follow to keep yourself alive. If caught in angelic form you could shift and die." I said.

Grace studied my words carefully.

"And shifting is what was happening to you right? Like when you got shot?" She asked.

Corn fields surrounded us on both the left and right side of the roads. We were coming up on a dirt road to the left. I signaled the blinker and went down the dirt road.

"Yes. If you shift you lose your abilities completely and die. Unlike your vessel, mine is ancient. It's been around for thousands of years. I've watched men fall and rise. If I was to shift I would surely turn into ash and die." I said.

The road was slightly bumpy on account of the potholes that filled the old dirt road. A rain must have come through recently and made the potholes bigger. We just needed somewhere to practice. Somewhere secluded, away from everybody and everything.

"But what about me?" Asked Grace.

"What about you?" I asked.

She was trying to wrap her head around all of this. The questions were good.

"I'm half human and half angel. Unlike you or anyone else." She said.

"Correct," I said.

"And... as far you know, there's no one else like me?" She asked.

"Correct again," I said.

"So, how can you be so sure, that I would even shift and die?" She asked.

I paused. I wasn't sure how to answer that. We were coming up on the spot I had picked out. To the right was a small thicket of wooded area that opened up into an open field of wheat. I pushed the cigar butt against the ashtray in the dash that had come with the vehicle when it was made.

"I suppose I'm not. But could you imagine the consequences? What if you were seen in your angelic form, flying about? What if people found out and decided to take you in for study? Imagine all the horrific things, those people might do." I said while bringing the car to a stop and putting it in park.

"I guess, I hadn't thought about that yet." Said Grace.

I took the keys out of the ignition and put them into my pocket and opened the driver's door. The sun was coming in through the open field. We had trees that lined and secluded our whereabouts from almost all directions. This field would be perfect. A rabbit made eye contact with me as I stood up from out of the car and it stayed perfectly still before running off back into the tall grass. The rabbit disappeared altogether a few seconds later.

I leaned my head back into the vehicle.

"Come on Grace, this is the spot. This is where you will learn to fly." I said.

She stepped out of the car, awaiting the next thing to do. Of course, it's easier to just demonstrate to her, her abilities. Abilities that I had given her. As her father at this moment, I had a duty to teach her just how truly special she was. I started to unbutton my shirt. Button by button I undid my shirt. My wings were eager to get out. Grace watched in curiosity as I let my wings out as they dropped to the ground. I rolled my shoulders in an upward motion. This brought my wings up, from dragging against the ground. I looked over my right and left shoulder and studied my wings for a brief second. I stretched my wings out. Up towards the sky. It was a freeing moment.

My charcoal-colored wings cast a shadow upon the ground. The sun was nearly three-quarters of the way done with its journey for the day.

I briefly thought of Rachel and stared down at the ground. My heart was heavy.

"I miss her too." Said Grace.

"How'd you know I was thinking of her?" I asked.

She shrugged her shoulders and briefly brought her hands up before dropping them back down to her side.

"I'm not sure. I just kind of sensed it. Plus you were looking at the ground for several seconds." Said Grace.

"Interesting. Can you do it on command?" I asked.

"Do what on command?" Asked Grace.

She bent down and grabbed a handful of grass she picked out of the ground. She studied each blade of grass as if they each had their own life force. The wind came through and blew them out of her hand, and she stood back up.

"Know what people are thinking," I said.

"Sometimes. I just started noticing it a few weeks ago." She said.

"So if I think of a number between one and one hundred, you'll be able to guess it?" I said amazed by what I was learning.

"Maybe. We can try and see if it works." Responded Grace.

I concentrated. I thought hard of a number. The number that came to mind was forty-seven. I repeated it in my head over and over.

"Forty-seven." Said Grace without skipping a beat.

"What the hell!" I said.

"Was I right?" She asked.

"Yes. You were right." I said.

We stood there for several minutes. Laughing and conjuring up different ways to test out her newfound ability. The wind started to slowly shift around us and blew the tall blades of grass in the opposite direction. A single feather from my wings came loose and onto the ground. Grace leaned down and picked it up. She carefully looked at it in the same manner that she did with the blades of grass before letting it go out of her hand and into the wind. She made eye contact with me.

"It's time isn't it?" She asked.

I nodded my head up and down.

"It is," I said.

She took off her shirt, exposing her wings. They were much smaller than mine. Of course that was a given. But the white purity of them was unmatched. Even my brother's wings weren't as white as hers.

"So you know how to retract and unretract them, yes?" I said.

She demonstrated her abilities. She quickly lowered her wings and raised them in the same fashion I had earlier. Her wings were young and youthful.

I pushed off the ground with my wings in a downward motion and started to hover off the ground a few feet.

"Grace if you do exactly as I just did you'll come up off the ground and hover. Just don't forget to flap your wings every so often, to keep you in the air." I said.

I moved over, in the air to Grace and extended my hands down to her hands.

"I'm scared." She said.

"There's nothing to be scared of darling. It's just you and I." I said while grabbing onto her hands.

She looked up at her wings that were now over her head. She moved her left wing and then her right wing.

"Grace," I said.

"Yes?" She replied.

"You got this," I said while still holding onto her hands and hovering in the air.

She closed her eyes and squeezed my hands ever so tightly. With one solid motion, she pushed her wings in a downward motion to the ground and quickly came up off the ground. Within seconds she was off in the air with me. She opened her eyes and was amazed. She smiled in the same fashion that her mother smiled. This was a moment, that we'd both remember, forever. It was like watching her first step. I wasn't there for any of that, but I was there for the first time she flew, and really that's all that mattered in this moment. She flapped her wings slightly every few seconds to stay off the ground.

"Lu?" She asked.

"Yes," I replied.

"How high can we go?" She asked.

I smiled. She was going to be just fine.

Morningstar Chapter 41

We landed back on the ground, near the SUV. Nobody had seen us during our flight. Halfway through Grace had ended up even letting go of my hands and flying all by herself. We both chuckled as we landed safely by the vehicle. The night sky had made itself known to both of us. The stars were out as was the moon.

"How long were we up there for?" Asked Grace.

I started to put my buttoned-up shirt back on and retract my feathers ever so slightly. Grace was already dressed.

"Time is irrelevant to us," I said.

"I think it's past my bedtime, Lu." She said while laughing.

"You're right, You're probably right." I said.

We got into the Traverse and I started the vehicle as we shut our doors. She buckled up, as did I. I couldn't stand to hear the seatbelt alarm go off, so I felt compelled to wear mine.

"That was a lot of fun." She said.

"It was," I said.

"Can we do it again sometime?" Asked Grace.

"Of course we can, anytime you want kiddo," I said.

I put the vehicle in reverse and began to back out of the field, back onto the dirt road we had ventured down.

"Just remember what I taught you and the rules I told you about," I said.

She stared over at me as I put the car into drive and began to make our way back into town. I just didn't want her to get caught.

"Don't get caught, I know." She said.

I looked over at her to make sure she knew the seriousness of what I was trying to explain to her.

"I won't get caught Lu, I pinky promise." She said as she held out her pinky for a pinky promise.

I interlaced my pinky with hers.

"Are you hungry?" I asked.

She let out a big yawn and stretched. We were back on the main road into Haven.

"Just tired." She said.

"You get some sleep. I'll let you know when we get home." I said.

She shut her eyes within seconds and leaned her head against the passenger door. She was out cold. Using that much physicality to fly takes a toll on the body. There were factors I had to keep in mind. After all, part of her was human. She needed to sleep more than me.

I PUT THE VEHICLE IN park. We had made it home. She was still out cold. I watched as she took in breaths and I ungripped the steering wheel and put the car in park. I wasn't about to wake her. I carefully unbuckled her from her seatbelt and came around to the passenger side. Her head was still leaned up against the door. I opened the door and caught her head from falling out. She instantly reached out to me and hugged me, still groggy and asleep. She held on. She was half-aware of what I was doing. I carried her inside to her bedroom. This wasn't a hard task to do at all. She weighed less than eighty pounds. Nothing for a fallen angel to lift. I opened the bedroom door and laid her carefully in her bed. Her covers were off to the side, and I covered her up so she could stay warm. I quietly tried to back out of the room before hearing her mumble something under her breath.

"What was that?" I asked.

"Good night Dad." She said.

My heart sank. She had just called me Dad. At this moment no correction was necessary. She had spoken from the heart.

"Good night my love." I said, as I shut the bedroom door.

The air stayed still as I made my way down the hallway down to the living room where Rachel had drawn her last breath. I stared down at the couch where she had died. There was nothing that could be done. Nothing I could do to bring her back. I started to tear up, before seeing a piece of paper that had caught my attention by the couch. It said "To Lu" On the paper. It was neatly folded. It was clearly Rachel's handwriting. I picked it up and unfolded the piece of paper and read it. It read:

"*To my creature of the night. My guardian angel. My lover. My Lu. If you are reading this I'm gone. Hopefully, everything is going okay. I felt like we could have been so much more, you and I. But out of what you and I were, came our beautiful daughter, Grace. I'm not the slightest bit worried that you'll take care of her and make sure you always do right by her and her best interest. Just remember I'm looking down on you two and will always be with you in times of need. Love always and forever, Rachel.*"

A single tear fell from my cheek onto the piece of paper. It smeared the ink on the piece of paper. It was nice to hear from her one last time.

"Hello Lucifer." Said someone from behind me.

I quickly turned around and gritted my teeth. It was Raphael.

"We need to talk brother." He said.

I wiped off my face to hide the fact from my brother that I had been crying.

"It's about Dad." He said.

Showing up like this unannounced had been happening for centuries. This wasn't an uncommon practice for Raphael. I crossed my arms.

"What about Dad?" I asked.

Raphael studied me intently and smiled a pure smile.

"He's requested again, that you fulfill your journey." He said.

"Of course he has." I said.

"You must leave, come first light for Eden." Said Raphael.

I chuckled.

"And If I don't?" I asked.

"We've already been through this." Said Raphael.

"I have a daughter to care for now brother. That you told me about." I said.

He moved a few steps closer to me.

"He told me you'd say that. The fact is this. You must return to Eden and partake of the fruit from the Tree." Said Raphael.

I grabbed my brother.

"But, If I do this I will die!" I shouted.

"You'll also perish if you don't partake of fruit from the Tree." Said, Raphael.

Raphael pushed away my hands off of him.

"Grace will be fine. I will keep an eye on her. Go and do this." He said while walking out the front door.

"And what if she's not?" I asked.

He turned around looking over his shoulder in my direction. The night sky was filled with the stars as I made my way onto the front porch.

"You have my word." He said.

Then just as quickly as he was there, he was gone. Up into the air he went until he was out of view.

I looked at the night sky in anger. I rubbed the top of my head.

"First light is it, Father? Fine, I'll leave for Eden in the first light. But you must make me a promise that you'll watch over my daughter. My daughter that you welcomed into this world." I said.

Just then a shooting star shot across the night sky.

I took it as a sign from him.

Morningstar Chapter 42

The location of Eden was a secret to the mortals of this realm. No one had discovered it's location. Some had come close but that was centuries ago. The exploration stage of man had come to an end, once technology had gripped its talons into them. Cellphones and computers everywhere have made it appear that humans knew of every location on Earth. Or so it appeared, the truth of it is, that they knew of every location but one. The Garden of Eden.

Wars have been fought and raged over the centuries many of which, I was either directly involved in or indirectly involved in. These wars took place close to The Garden. The secret location remained intact, except to a select few celestial beings. Those beings that I was aware of were Michael, Raphael, Gabriel, and myself.

The morning sun had started to shine through the windows of the house.

I didn't sleep. Or my version of sleep at least. I couldn't. I had checked on Grace several times throughout the night, just to make sure she was okay and sleeping soundly. Other than that I had made preparations. Preparations for the long journey ahead. I had already drank a few cups of coffee that I had prepared throughout the night. My energy and strength were at peak levels. The caffeine would sustain me enough for the journey throughout the day and night. I had accounted for a day and night travel based on our current location in Kansas.

"What do you mean you have to leave me?" Said Grace, in a sharp tone.

Her hands were on her hips as she stood up from the table and pushed her bowel back away from her cereal.

"It won't be for long, I just have to do this one thing," I said while rubbing the top of my head.

How much could I honestly tell her without telling her? What could she comprehend, and not comprehend? All these questions came rushing through my head.

"You promised Mom! You even promised me that you'd never leave me!" Said Grace, while stomping away down the hallway to her room.

Within a matter of seconds, she had slammed her bedroom door shut.

I followed her down the hallway where I had gotten her bedroom door to the face. I laid my hand against the doorknob and grasped it slightly.

"Grace, hunny?" I said.

A muffled response was heard through the door.

"Go away, Lu!" I heard from the other side of the bedroom door.

"I can't lie to you Grace, okay? I'll tell you what is going on." I said.

No noise could be heard coming from the other side of the door. All of a sudden the pitter-patter of feet shuffling could be heard and the doorknob jiggled out of my hand and turned. I was approached by a pissed-off four-foot-something half-angel with a temper from hell. She crossed her arms and stared up at me, with her eyebrows slanted downwards. This showed me that she was beyond angry at our breakfast conversation.

"You going to tell me or?" She said, still standing there full of sass and attitude.

"It's just that–," I said before being interrupted.

"It's not that simple?" She snapped back.

I cowered down. I had never met my match before but I was for sure feeling about two feet tall right about now to this little girl.

"It's not that simple," I said while blowing out air through my nostrils.

The door slammed once against in my face.

"You make me so angry Lu." She said from the other side of the bedroom door.

"Fine! You want the truth! I have to go to Eden. The Garden. Now I don't know how much you do, or don't know about Eden but I have to go, because it's Dad's orders to go!" I said while letting out a breath.

I had said it pretty loud. Loud enough that it might be considered shouting to some. The pitter-patter and shuffling of feet moving could be heard again coming from the other side of the bedroom door. I was met by a different little girl. She had changed her demeanor altogether.

"So, can I go with you to Eden?" She asked innocently.

I leaned down to get eye level with her and rested my hands on her shoulders.

"Honestly, no. But only because I have to keep you safe here, while I go do this." I said.

She looked worried and confused.

"But then, who's going to watch me while you are gone?" She asked.

Before I could take a breath in to respond a voice from behind us, down the hallway to the entrance of the house responded.

"I am." Said the familiar voice.

Grace carefully backed back into her room while I shielded her and blocked the entrance of her room.

"Be not afraid you two." Said the voice as the shadow of the voice came into the house.

The shadow appeared to be big, bigger than a human to say the least. This shadow also had what appeared to be four wings.

"Ah, Lucifer I see you are ready for your travels." Said the voice as the figure rounded the hallway and made themselves known.

It was Ralphel. His bottom two wings dragged slightly against the floor, making a shuffling noise as he took steps from one foot to the other.

"And Grace, I'm sorry but we have not met yet." Said Ralphel as he looked directly at me.

"Who is it?" Asked Grace.

I leaned my head into the bedroom while still standing guard in the doorframe.

"It's your uncle," I said.

This made her curious. Rachel didn't have any siblings or living family members. That much I knew on account of the funeral and our prior talks within our relationship. This was an eye-opener for Grace. To have another family member, one on her father's side even, would surely make her happy. She popped out her head from inside the bedroom and looked passed me down the hallway at Ralphel.

"Hello, Grace." Said Raphael bowing in a noble gesture as a sign of respect.

"Hi. What's your name?" She said as she smiled and stuck her head even further outside the door.

She had wedged herself between me and the doorframe so she could get a better look at Raphael.

Raphael stopped bowing and looked up at her.

"You have your mother's eyes, dear. My name is Raphael. I am your uncle." Said Raphael.

This made her smile for a split second. She was flattered. I moved out of her way, now that I knew his intentions weren't in the slightest bit malicious.

"You have four wings, how cool is that!" She said with excitement.

Raphael chuckled slightly and put his hands on his hips as he brought his wings up slowly to show them off to her. His plated armor that he wore showed our reflection from clear down the hallway about fifteen or more feet from us.

"I heard you had wings as well." Said Raphael.

Grace ran back into her room and threw her shirt off, exposing her wings. She had them retracted slightly. They fell to her knees from behind. The white purity of their color was mesmerizing to look at. It reminded me of my wings before I had been cast out.

"Here's mine!" She said, pushing passed me in the hallway and doing a little spin move to show hers off.

"All three of us have wings!" She said.

"Yes, we do," I said.

"Indeed. I love yours." Said Raphael.

BEEP

The watch on my left wrist chimed to let me know it was seven in the morning. The sunlight was quickly pouring in from the east side of the house. I was wearing a black shirt, some jeans, and some square-toe boots.

"Lucifer. You look–. Well, you look nice." Said Raphael.

He was very clearly lying and not amused by my appearance. I couldn't care less. He and I didn't have many issues with each other. But apparently, a fashion sense was one of them in his book.

"Well you look like a dork, so," I said while pulling a cigar from my right pocket and lighting it up with a zippo lighter I had found in the house.

The inhale of smoke filled my lungs. I pushed it out in such a manner to float above Grace's head and push towards Raphael's face. Raphael quickly threw his hands up in the air in a waving motion to clear the smoke from around him.

"He looks great, Lu!" Said Grace excitedly.

This made Raphael smile. He smirked ever so slightly.

"Thank you, Grace." Said Raphael.

She quickly ran down the hallway to him, wings out and all. Her wings fluttered slightly as she got closer to him. She reached out for his hand and he met her halfway as she started to try and pull him down the hallway towards me.

"Come see my room, Uncle Raphael!" She said.

I got out of the way as she pulled him into her bedroom. Raphael made eye contact with me as he went by me into the bedroom.

"This is my room. This is where I hang out, do schoolwork, play with my toys, and listen to music!" Said Grace, still excited by his presence.

"Grace, this is wonderful. You can show me all this and more as we get to know each other. Do I have your permission to be your babysitter while Lucifer is gone?" He asked.

"Fine by me! You just got to take it up with him." She said while digging through her stuffed animals and pointing in my general direction by the doorway.

I took another hit off of my cigar. The taste of clover filled my throat. Surprisingly Raphael didn't fit well in her room. Especially with his four wings. He showed mild discomfort as he turned around to face me.

Not because of her or myself, but because his wings were bumping into things variously placed throughout the room.

"It's time." Said Raphael looking at me.

I looked down at Grace and then back up at him.

"Okay," I said while nodding.

Grace was still busy digging out stuffed animals to show her newly hired babysitter and Uncle. He smiled at her as she pulled out a stuffed angel with wings. It was small and brittle.

"This can be Mommy! We can all play together and go flying!" She said.

My heart. I could feel the emotions of my heart hurting from missing Rachel. As for Grace, she was the very definition of being innocent.

The pink paint job of the room mixed with the stuffed animal pile, and the angel reference brought a few tears to my eyes.

"Grace I think Lu, has to go." Said Raphael.

"Oh right!" She said.

"When will you be back?" Asked Grace.

Her wings now fluttered from being overjoyed and preoccupied. Her back was still turned away from me as she continued to dig through her stuffed animal pile.

"Should be back before the end of the night or early morning tomorrow," I said.

"You pinky-promise?" She said as she hurried over to pass Raphael and to the doorway where I was standing.

She had extended her right-hand pinky finger out in my direction.

"I pinky promise," I said while interlocking my pinky with her pinky.

"Okay! Have fun in Eden!" She said.

I looked over at Raphael who had just watched our conversation and the way we interacted with each other very carefully.

He nodded his head, as did I in each other's general direction.

"You be safe out there." Said Raphael in a concerned tone.

"You watch over her," I said while taking a final drag from my clover cigar.

"I will." He said.

I took one final look at my daughter. She took one final look at me. We locked eyes for a few seconds.

"Goodbye Grace," I said while holding back hidden tears in my eyes.

"Goodbye, Lu." She said smiling at me for a brief second before going back to playing with her toys.

That was it. I knew this was more than likely going to be the last time I saw my daughter. Raphael knew as well. But I knew she was safe as long as he was there. I made my way to the outside, through the broken front door. I threw the cigar butt onto the grass and stomped it out with my boot. With no neighbors in sight, I took off my shirt and let out of my wings. I thrusted myself into the air and off I went to The Garden of Eden.

Morningstar Chapter 43.

Eden[1]. / (ˈiːdən) / noun. *Also called: Garden of Eden Old Testament the garden in which Adam and Eve were placed at the Creation. a delightful place, region, dwelling, etc; paradise*

It is also called in Genesis "the garden of the Lord" (the God of Israel) and in Ezekiel "the garden of God." The term Eden probably is derived from the Akkadian word edinu, borrowed from the Sumerian Eden, meaning "plain".

I had been flying for quite some time. High above the clouds where nobody could see me. I knew I was headed in the right general direction. Regardless of being kicked off Eden, and falling from the heavens, I still had my angelic sense about me. As I had mentioned earlier, a handful of us knew of the whereabouts of the mysterious unknown Garden of Eden.

According to Genesis (2:4–3:24), God created Adam from the dust of the ground and then planted the Garden of Eden with the "tree of life" and the forbidden "tree of the knowledge of good and evil" at its center. God tasked Adam with tending the garden and naming the animals therein and gave him the single command to not eat the fruit of the tree of the knowledge of good and evil. Lacking a helper for his work, Adam was put into a deep sleep while God took from him a rib and created a companion, Eve. The two were persons of innocence and lived unashamedly without clothes as husband and wife.

All lights had been gone for hours. I was flying in pitch darkness. No sign of civilization could be seen from below as I made my way just below the clouds.

"You cut me off. You made me what I am. You gave me free choice in the garden to tempt Eve. I suppose I didn't disappoint." I said out loud to the heavens as if Father was listening.

My senses were becoming heightened. I felt pulled to the east. So I changed my direction and began to head east. My wings were becoming heavy. I knew I was close. A small mountain range started to appear from down below. Nothing but bare desert. Not a tree, or even wildlife for that matter made itself known to me as I started my descent through the clouds onto the ground. The rest I would have to make on foot. I touched down near the mouth of a large river. I knew I was in the right spot. Water came from four directions and intersected. Not only did I touch down near the mouth of a large river, I had landed on a ledge to oversee my surroundings. Around me was a mountain range. I was in the Middle East. A mixture of dirt and sand blew up and slightly slapped me against the face. I was on the outskirts of Eden. The water that came from four directions, represented four different river systems that intersected perfectly in the middle of this barren desert. If I followed the northern river system I'd run smack down into The Garden of Eden.

Off in the distance, a figure appeared. A single storm cloud hung over this figure. No light from the sun could seem to break through the large dark storm cloud. I had to address whomever it was. They had already started to make their way towards me. I had one of two options, fly or walk. Nothing of mortal descent should be out here. So I knew I didn't need to be too cautious. I took off flying low to the ground. I flapped my wings ever so often to stay up in the air. The figure was further off than I had expected.

The sky started to become dark and the air was full of the smell of sulfur. I was underneath the storm cloud. My shadow quickly disappeared from the ground. I was quite a ways away from the four intersecting river bodies that I had seen from the mountain ledge I had stood upon.

The figure hailed me to touch down as it continued to walk towards me. It was a female. Her hands were up on her hips as she waited for me to touch down. I was within a few feet of her. A bellowed voice came from beneath the storm cloud and mildly chuckled.

"Lucifer. Honey. Oh how I've missed your stench." Said the unknown female figure.

She appeared slightly disfigured. Regardless of the disfigurements she was still seductive in a nature. She wore black cloth. Every bit of clothing was skin tight on her body.

I knew exactly who it was as she smiled at me. Within a matter of seconds she was within a few feet from my face.

"Hello, Lilith." I said.

Morningstar Chapter 44

The storm cloud that was overhead raged a violent tune. Lighting cracked across the sky and thunder followed. The ground was beyond dry. It was cracked. The surface hadn't seen rain in centuries. Lilith looked me up and down like I was a snack with her hands still on her hips.

"How long has it been Lucifer?" She asked while circling around me.

"And what on Earth brings you back here?" She asked while rubbing her sharp teeth with her tongue.

I cleared my throat before responding. The dry climate had made itself known to me. I knew if I was going to survive this encounter with a succubus I had to choose my words carefully. There was no escaping her at this point. I couldn't just fly or walk away.

"It's been a minute," I said while pulling a clover cigar and lighting it.

I took a long drag off of the cigar and blew the smoke into the air. Lilith walked through the smoke and grabbed the cigar from out of my hand. She too took a drag off of my cigar and blew it into my face.

"You don't write to me, call me, email me. What's a woman gotta do to get a little attention?" Said Lilith while circling me.

She seemed to defy gravity itself. Her body lightly levitated off the ground. She went in a circle around me repeatedly before stopping inches away from my face.

"Must have slipped my mind," I said.

"Yet here you are now. Lucifer Morningstar." She said, taking another hit off of the cigar and blowing it into my face.

I was slightly annoyed. I was fairly certain I had a thing to do elsewhere. It was like I was drawn to her, as soon as I saw the storm cloud. This wasn't my first run-in with her. We had a history. A history I didn't want to necessarily repeat. She threw the cigar down to the ground. I briefly looked down at it, as it was extinguished below her. She was inches from my face. She smiled.

"Want to have sex?" She asked without skipping a beat.

Her hand had begun to explore my chest and neck. She twirled the tip of her darkened fingernail that was razor sharp against my throat ever so carefully. I grabbed the exploring hand of hers by the wrist and gave her no attention other than to push it away from my throat.

"No thanks," I said.

"Oh, but Lucifer. You and me. Could you imagine? I imagine it all the time." She said.

She turned around, with her back towards me and leaned down.

"You could take me here and now Lucifer. Just you and I. A fallen for a fallen. Oh, imagine the fun we'd have." She said looking back at me.

"I already told you, no thanks," I said.

She snarled her teeth at me and rolled her long tongue. She wasn't happy with my responses.

"Fine! You never could deliver anyways, you fallen piece of trash!" She screamed.

Her voice seemed to echo in all directions and find its way back to my ears tenfold.

"What can I say, I've just never been your type," I said.

She levitated further into the air, still keeping an eye on me.

"Typical. Just like Adam. He couldn't understand either. He just wanted me to submit." She snarled.

"But do I have news for you." She said while landing back down on the ground in front of me.

"Oh?" I said.

At this point, if I made a run for it she would surely track me down and attempt to kill me. She had no side. No good or bad, just Lilith's side. That was the only side that mattered to her. I had to keep the conversation light and moving in such a way that she would get bored of me and let me be on my way.

"I require a general. You fit the bill darling. You'd make a fine general. I'm taking the fight to him." She said.

"Him?" I asked.

"Yes, him. Father. The bastard that created me and you. The one that made me and you without a purpose. Well I've got news for him, I've found my purpose." She said.

Her eyes were blackened by the years of being what she was. After all, she was cast from The Garden of Eden. She was Adam's first wife. She was created from the same dirt as he was. After she didn't submit to her husband, Adam and Father became impatient with her and cast her out of the Garden.

"You making Eve curious in the Garden about the fruit was only the beginning. Making her partake of the fruit was all part of my plan from the very beginning." She said while chuckling.

My eyes widened. Was she admitting to the very thing that I had gone down for? Was she the one to blame?

"What are you saying, Lilith?" I asked.

"What I'm saying is this. While Dad has turned a blind eye towards me. I've been gathering my masses. Men around the world. Fallen angels. Spies. You name it. All together for one cause. To take him down once and for all." She said.

"So you have a following?" I said.

All the while the storm cloud brewed wickedness and darkness overhead. Lightning continued to crack across the sky.

"A following? No, my darling. I have a fucking army!" She said with excitement.

I pulled out my last cigar out of my pocket. She quickly took it from me.

"Have a light?" She said.

I pulled out the zippo I had used at the house earlier in Kansas and flicked open the lid and rubbed my thumb against the ignitor and a small flame cast upon her shadow and the surrounding darkness. She inhaled as she carefully kept the cigar above the lighter. I shook my wings. I was becoming restless with this conversation and the games she was playing.

"All I'm saying is, consider this. A place at my table. With me, not against me. A fallen angel kicked out of Heaven, and the first woman kicked out of Eden, taking on the creator." She said while blowing out smoke into the air.

I knew at this point I needed to say, whatever she needed to hear to get her to leave me alone. This whole talk about an army and me joining as a general was crazy.

"I'll consider it," I said.

This instantly piqued her interest.

"I'll be in touch then." She said while giving me back the half-smoked cigar.

"How will I know when you need to get ahold of me?" I asked while throwing the cigar down onto the ground.

"You'll know." She said moving in closer to my face.

She extended her mouth to my mouth and connected with my lips. She shook slightly as she continued to stay connected to my lips with hers.

"Until next time." She said as she pulled away and started to walk away from me.

And that was that. Within seconds the sun started to shine through, and the storm cloud that was overhead quickly dissipated as

I looked up and was welcomed by the heat of the Sun. I looked back down in her general direction and she was nowhere to be found. It's as if it had never happened.

I chuckled and shook my head. I made my way back to where I was. Back to the mouth of the intersecting four rivers. Where I knew the Garden was. I was on a mission from Dad.

Regardless of the circumstances, I wasn't about to revolt against him. I had a little girl to watch out for now. Out of all the people in the world, that little girl needed me the most.

Morningstar Chapter 45

The Garden of Eden wasn't a physical place that could be found with the eyes. It was a place that needed to be felt with the heart.

I took a few steps forward surrounded by the intersecting waters of the rivers that were around me. All around me the water connected in such a fashion that it ran north, south, east, and west.

I was here. All I needed to do now was believe I was there. I kneeled by the loose soil next to one of the rivers. I dug my hands deep into the dirt and closed my eyes. I squeezed the dirt with all my might and chanted an ancient angelic prayer. My eyelids started to vibrate and my whole body started to shake. It became bitter cold. I was crossing over into the unseen. The spiritual realm. Flashes of a flaming sword and a multitude of wings could be seen in my mind while my eyes remained closed. It was the gatekeeper of Eden. Jophiel. One of my brothers.

I could feel the heat from the flaming sword as it danced in and out of the vision that I was having. Jophiel was guarding the gate of Eden with the sword given to him by Father to drive out Adam and Eve. I was at his mercy. The smell of ash and brimstone filled my nostrils. He had the upper hand. I was merely knocking at the gate. I continued to chant not in the old angelic tongue but merely in plain English.

"By the sweat of your face you shall eat bread, till you return to the ground, for out of it you were taken; for you are dust, and to dust you shall return," I said out loud. {**Genesis 3:19**}

THE FLAME FROM THE sword moved closer to the vision that I was having. Everything was becoming more clear. I could make out my brother Jophiel completely now. His voice could be heard speaking out to me.

"How dare you come here Lucifer Morningstar. Your curse was clear when you were cast out. You are forbidden to cross this plain. You were meant to walk the Earth for all its entirety!" Shouted Jophiel.

His voice was deep, and much older sounding than my other brothers.

I could taste his blade. He was blocking me from entering. My body continued to convulse in the earthly realm. He felt no pity for me or the reason I was there.

I bowed my head. Showing that I meant no ill will. A sign of respect among angels.

"Brother I am here on Father's orders," I said moments before the blade was going to connect with my neck.

He pulled me through. To the spiritual realm. The same realm that separated mortals from Heaven. Within seconds, flashes of lights could be seen as my wings were forced out. Shortly after my hands were extended outwards as I saw trillions of stars and planets and finally a blinding bright light. The light started to fade. I felt a hand swiftly upon my shoulder as I continued to kneel. It was Jophiel.

"He told me you'd come. Although I don't agree with it. I just had to make sure you knew the reason." Said Jophiel as he pulled his hand away from my shoulder when I looked up at him.

"Rise Lucifer. Rise and do what you must. Just remember the reason for which you are here." Said Jophiel.

His multitude of wings had disappeared entirety. He had just a single set of white majestic wings. His golden armor glistened off an unknown light source as he sheathed his flaming sword. His appearance hadn't changed one bit. He had a much older face than any of us, however. His blue eyes watched me carefully.

"Figured you'd be happy to see me," I said, as I got to my feet and lowered my wings and arms.

He let out a low groan as he bit his tongue from saying anything. His sense of humor hadn't changed one bit either.

There was no sky here, only white light, surrounding the both of us in all directions. I took a look around. Before me was my very unusually tall brother, Jophiel. Behind him was a black gate made of magical iron that wasn't made by man's hand. This gate was the entryway into Eden. Behind me and to my left and right was nothing but whiteness. I couldn't see more than a few feet away from me. The only path that lay in front of me was the one into The Garden. Passed the colossus-size black ironed gate.

"You know where to go. The place where it all started." Said Jophiel.

He put his hands together in a clapping fashion that echoed all around us.

The walls that were connected to the gate went on for miles in both directions. Trying to explain the vastness of how tall and how long the walls are, is impossible. Just know this was the only entryway in and out of The Garden of Eden.

Moments after he clapped his hands the gate started to lift out of the ground. The very ground that we stood upon shook. He pointed towards the gate.

"Go, now, and partake, as Father has asked of you." Said Jophiel.

He ushered me in such a way that signaled me to head inside. At this point, the lifting of the gate had completely stopped. The ground stopped shaking.

No sign of emotion could be made out by his facial expressions. There were no expressions. It was as if he was nothing more than an empty vessel.

"Go. Now." He said once more.

I took a deep breath and retracted my wings slightly. I started to walk forward passing my brother who had stepped out of the way. I was really about to do this. The shifting process had already happened to me earlier when I was shot, but caffeine fixed that. When I left the bar in Tennessee, I also started to shift when I came across Gabriel. By his sacrifice of falling to his death, I was saved and my powers were restored. But this? This would be the end of me.

I looked back behind me as the gate seemed to fade in and out and disappear altogether. I was inside. Back in Eden.

Morningstar Chapter 46

Within seconds the gate disappeared from my view. That's when I noticed it. The absence of sound. Noises could not be heard by my ears. A yellow aura filled my vision as I saw the field of trees. One stood high among all the rest. The Tree of Knowledge. This was the very tree that I had told Eve indirectly all those centuries ago to partake from. The very reason I had been forced out of Heaven. Maybe I was a lost cause for what I had done. Maybe I had no purpose. This would be my final resting place. I walked studying each tree almost identical to the next one. Their lush green leaves blew in the wind. However, no rustling of the leaves on the trees could be heard.

"And now I'm here. Doing as you wish. I'm asking you that you reconsider what you are asking of me." I said out in the open.

It was the only noise that could be heard. Lush green fields of grass blew ever so softly in the ominous wind. Trees could be seen for miles. Each one with its distinct fruit and color. The only thing that kept crossing my mind was Grace. I needed her to be okay. I wanted to believe she was okay. I trembled as I made the climb up the hill to The Tree of Knowledge. But I wasn't going to back down. It was either partake of the fruit of the Forbidden Tree or shift and die. It was a double-edged sword.

Each step up the grassy hill seemed to be harder than the last step. The caffeine had worn off. Raphael would continue to keep an eye on Grace. I imagined them playing with the stuffed animals together and slightly chuckled. I was genuinely smiling. Tears however, filled my vision. This next part would be the hardest thing I had ever done. Could I lay down my life and end it all?

I made it to the top of the hill and looked up. The Forbidden Tree stood proudly in front of me. The tree's leaves had an emerald glimmer to them. It stood out differently than all the rest. Down below I could make out where I had come in from. The gate didn't seem to fade away up here on the hill.

I turned my focus to the tree. I was tired. Tired of running. Tired of hiding. Tired of just being tired. With my hands extended, I reached out and grabbed the most luscious piece of fruit from The Tree of Knowledge. Its radiant red color glistened in the vastness of the soundless, sunless environment I was in. One bite is all it would take. My life started to flash before my eyes.

"That'll be $5.45 please." Said Rachel.

"I thought it was on the house?" I said confusingly.

Rachel smiled and laughed while standing behind the cash register of the coffee shop.

"Okay but just this once, Lu." Said Rachel.

I took a sip of the freshly poured caffeinated drink this beauty of a creature had made for me. It was hot and delicious.

"Oh, where do you think you're going?" Said Rachel with her hands on her hips and pointing her finger at her lips.

This drove me wild. Utter bliss.

"You didn't think I'd forget your kiss did you?" I asked her.

She continued to stand behind the counter, stoically.

"Come here you." She said.

We embraced and time itself stood still. Just her and I. Noting could stop us, nothing could stand in our way.

I flashed back out of it.

The piece of red fruit was grasped in my fingers inches away from my mouth. I started to open my mouth to take a bite. I pulled it away from my face and closed my mouth. My body was trembling. I was flashing back again. This time the vision was stronger.

"This sure is good ice cream!" Shouted Grace.

"It's the best," I said to her.

She took a large lick off of her single-dip waffle cone and smiled at me.

"You know you're not half bad Lu." Said Grace, while taking another lick of her ice cream.

I took a lick of my mint chocolate chip ice cream cone and made eye contact with Grace.

"You're not half bad yourself kiddo," I said.

I snapped back out of it. All my memories were flashing before my eyes and I hadn't even taken a bite out of the fruit. My body continued to tremble. That's when I felt it in my mouth. I looked down at the back side of the piece of fruit that I was holding in my right hand. A chunk had gone missing from the fruit. I moved my jaw up and down and felt something within my mouth. It was the missing chunk. I tried to spit it out but it was too good. Before I could open my mouth I had swallowed the chewed-up bite.

My life was flashing before my eyes because I was dying. I tried to raise my wings and couldn't. The weight of them made me feel weak. I was shifting. I dropped the fruit down to the ground and watched it disappear into the grassy ground. I looked up above the Tree.

"There! Is that what you wanted?" I shouted as I fell to my knees.

I knew it was only a matter of time before I drew my last breath. As I knelt the tears flowed down my cheeks and onto the ground. No more memories came to me. I was alone here and I was dying.

A few moments went by before I realized a figure that was standing between me and The Tree of Knowledge. A blinding bright light overtook my vision. I held my hand up to try and see who the figure was, in between my fingertips it became more clear.

It was Rachel.

Morningstar Chapter 47

The blinding bright light subsided in front of the tree. It was my beloved Rachel, but she was different. She hovered in mid-air before coming down onto the ground. She had wings! Beautiful, majestic wings. She had on pure white clothes as she gracefully stepped towards me. Her hair was long and flowing. It took every bit of strength to look up at her. The digestion of the piece of fruit was already causing me to shift. Soon the process would be complete. I faded in and out as she kneeled by my face. My eyes were becoming heavy.

"Rache–" I said before gasping for another breath of air.

She kneeled in such a fashion that she could cradle my head in her lap. I could feel the warmth of her as she touched my face ever so gently with her hands.

"My poor Lu." She said as she continued to caress the side of my face.

I tried to talk but nothing came out. Mostly mumbles of words that wouldn't make sense to anybody. If this was the way I was going to die, seeing her in her angelic form was pure bliss. I was with my love. My body was failing on me.

"Your time isn't finished in the mortal realm." Said Rachel while studying my eyes.

Her beautiful blue eyes connected with mine and our souls started to dance as we studied each other's eyes. All was silent.

"You have to return to our baby girl." Said Rachel as she started to lean her lips down towards mine.

With what strength I had left I pushed my lips upwards towards hers. Our lips connected. At that moment I took a breath. I felt as if my strength was being slowly restored to me. My brain told me I needed another kiss. So that's exactly what I did. I grabbed the back of her head, pulled her in while still lying in her lap, and connected our lips again. It felt as if we were one again. Her wings came up and blocked out the whiteness of the cloudless sky that was around us. With what strength I had restored to my body I came up off the ground and drew out my wings. Her lips stayed connected to mine as well as her hands as she helped pull me up. She pushed me away for a moment. She was full of smiles, as was I. I was no longer shifting. Her angelic kiss had saved me. I felt like I was extremely powerful, not only that, caffeinated beyond comprehension. With our hands still grasping each other's, my wings came up to meet hers and we touched the tip of our wings together.

"Lu, I can only give you so much time." She said in a slight panic.

"What do you mean?" I asked.

"My kiss will only work for a few hours in the mortal realm." She said dropping her wings to her wayside.

"What did you mean it wasn't my time to go?" I asked dropping my wings to my side as well.

"You need to hurry! You need to get back to Grace before it's too late." She said loudly.

"But why? Rachel, you need to tell me what's going on!" I said.

She closed her eyes and started to tremble ever so slightly. She pulled back her hands and put them in a praying position in front of her while still keeping her eyes locked on me.

"Because, Raphael, is back in Heaven as of about a few minutes ago, even though time doesn't apply up there. His orders were to leave Grace, unattended so Michael can–." She said before stopping all together.

I took a step towards her and grabbed her hands once more and looked into her eyes.

"So Michael can what?" I asked.

She was very clearly upset but remained confident in her angelic form.

"Michael is going to kill our baby! Our baby girl is going to be murdered on orders from above. Michael thinks our girl is a monster that must be taken out of the world and has no place in it." She said as a few tears came out of her eyes.

"What!" I shouted.

"I know that you will do everything to protect her. The path was simple. Partake of the fruit and shift and die, then Michael could easily kill our daughter!" She said.

"How long do I have?" I asked as I clenched my fists into a ball.

"Hours. Just enough to get back and confront Michael. No more, no less." She said.

I was filled with rage. That monster of a brother wanted a fight, then that's exactly what he would get.

"Don't cloud your judgment. You know what you must do." Said Rachel as she caressed the side of my face with her hand down to my chin.

I embraced Rachel again.

"Go now." She said as she gently pushed me away from her.

"I'll keep her safe," I said as I walked backward a few steps.

She nodded with approval as she gracefully leaped into the air and hovered in midair as I started my descent back down the hill of the Tree.

With powers restored once more, and knowing I only had hours to spare, I ran. I ran with all my might back towards the entrance of the gates of Eden.

I had one final task. One final drive to push me. I jumped into the air and extended out my wings. I was flying above the trees towards the entrance at top speed. Within a few seconds, I'd be back at the entryway.

"I'm coming, Grace. Daddy's coming." I said.

Chapter 48 of Morningstar

I HAD MADE IT. I WAS back in Kansas. Back at the driveway of the house. The house was in ruins. Between the front door being smashed to bits by me earlier, when I had kicked it in, to take care of Josh, and Michael descending through the living room, it had looked as if a tornado had just ripped right through Rachel and Grace's house. I knew what he was after. He was going after Grace. I had seen him descend, wings down in a violent manner so he could break through the ceiling as if he were a knife slicing through butter. My strength was leaving me, I could feel it being pulled away from me with each step up the driveway that I took. Each step felt heavier than the last. I didn't know how much time I had left, all I knew was I needed to get to Grace. I needed to stop Michael. Rachel's angelic kiss would only last so long with me. Soon I would indeed shift and die. But not without stopping Michael. He always longed to please Father so much. But not today, not at this moment. I had flown for so many thousands of miles to get back here.

"Michael!" I screamed at the top of my lungs.

It could be heard for miles around. Rage was coursing through my vessel. I knew I could use this to my advantage. After all, I had thousands of years of rage built up in my system. I thrived on it.

"Get your ass out here!" I hollered.

Time stood still. Distant cars on the nearby road by the mailbox were frozen in time, not moving an inch. I knew this time, that Grace wouldn't be affected by its time-stopping abilities. He didn't have a soul to ascend, he was there for one thing and one thing only.

My fists were clenched. I knew he had heard me. I heard the loud thudding of him coming up to the front doorway, that I was standing at.

"Grace you okay hunny?" I asked.

At first, there was no answer. My heart sank. If he had harmed a hair on her head, I was going to kill him.

A faint voice from the back bedroom could be heard. It was Grace.

"I'm okay. I'm–just scared." Said Grace in a muffled manner.

She must have been hiding, somewhere in the house. I picked up on this on account of her voice being so faint and muffled.

Michael had approached the doorway during this time. He was in full armor. From head to toe. The clanking could be heard from his armored boots as he stared me down. Her talking instantly got his attention. He turned away from me, with his back towards me, and started to head back inside the house.

"Hey! You and me Michael!" I said.

I walked up the steps to the house. I channeled my rage. I flapped my wings upwards, which catapulted me forward, towards him. I was going to hit him dead on, with his back turned. The gusting noise of my wings alerted him. Michael turned around at the last second before contact and slapped me away as if I were a fly. I was launched backward onto the front lawn. My body tore into the ground. My mind went elsewhere. I instantly thought of the time, I fell from Heaven. The impact that I had left. I came back too, my body still tumbling in the dirt. I gripped the ground with my hands and launched myself back towards the house.

"Enough Lucifer. You know what must be done." Said Michael.

He was walking back into the house further. His head went from left to right. The metallic gold helmet shined in the setting of the sun. A single gleam shined into my eyes from his helmet. He was looking for her.

I fell to my knees. Not in despair, but in weakness. The blow had landed its mark upon me. My brother was barely trying at this point. Soon he would find her hiding spot. I needed to get into his head. I needed to be a trickster. My specialty. I stood to my knees wiping off the dirt from my face and eyelids. Clumps of dirt fell to the ground from my face and hands. I felt the warmness in my saliva. I was bleeding. I spit blood out of my mouth onto the ground and watched it soak into the dirt and grass.

I chuckled. Laughter was an emotion I had learned to master. A deep belly laugh filled my lungs and an outburst of laughter bellowed out for miles.

I walked towards the house. One step after another.

"You know why Dad has never praised you, brother?" I said while still laughing.

I still saw him searching around in the main hallway of the house, by the front door. His armored boots clanked on the floor with each step that he took. He flipped over the couch in the living room and sent it flying into the drywall.

"Because you were the weakest of all of us. You always have been. You call yourself an archangel? You're a washed up, has been. You're nothing in his eyes! You're just like me!" I shouted.

"I'm nothing like you!" Screamed Michael.

He now was facing me. His wings were arched out. I could tell I had set him off. His golden armor was magnificent. It shimmered in the setting of the Kansas sunlight. His sword remained in its sheathe on his right side.

"I've always been his favorite. It was never you Lucifer. You call yourself brother yet you've always put yourself above others, you've even put yourself above him." Said Michael.

"You want to please him? Then put an end to all of this once and for all. I bet you, can't even win in a fight against me!" I said.

I spit more blood out of my mouth and wiped the excess from my lips. I lifted my wings up into the air. I looked to my left and right, the blackness of my wings put a shadow on the ground that I took in for a second. We were built by the same creator. The same father. If he could make me bleed my blood, I could make him bleed his as well. He was irritated. I could tell. I was getting to him.

"You're a disgrace in his eyes because you don't even have the guts to kill me," I said.

A laugh bellowed from my lungs.

"I'm the favorite," I said while stepping into the doorframe of the house.

"Take another step and die." Said Michael drawing his sword from its sheathe.

"I would gladly die for her, a thousand times over if it meant protecting her," I said while taking another step.

The last step I felt as if my life force was being drained. I didn't care. I knew the shifting process was almost complete. Soon I would be a mortal. I would turn to ash and nothing but a pile of ash would remain on the ground.

"Then die." Said Michael.

He lunged the sword deep into my chest, twisting as he went into my chest cavity. I felt the collapse of my heart. I could feel the pain scorching through my body. It felt as if I was being burnt alive. I could see the vengeance in my brother's eyes. My eyes started to drift. The scorching pain was the only thing keeping me conscious. Blood began to pool out my mouth.

"You–can't–." I said trying to speak.

I grabbed onto Michael's shoulders trying to hold myself upright.

"CAN'T WHAT? KILL HER? She's an abomination. Like you. An unloved, tainted creation that should have never existed." Said Michael.

He had dug his foot into my knee. He hugged me only to push off of me and pull his sword out in an upward motion. I collapsed. I instantly fell to the ground. A pool of blood is all I saw. I gurgled up warm blood and it drooled out from my bottom lip.

"But–." I gurgled up more blood.

"But what, Lucifer? You're shifting, it is over." Said Michael.

I grabbed at his feet. Pulling with what strength I had left. It wasn't much, but I still had words to say.

"I–love–her," I said.

My hands let go of his feet. He wasn't within reach anymore. Blood was gushing out of the hole he had left in my chest. Red was all I saw around me. It couldn't be stopped. There was no angelic healing. No caffeine could fix this. I knew it too. In the back of my head, I knew I was almost dead. The only thing that I wanted to make sure of, was that she was safe.

I mustered up the strength to pray.

"Father. I call on you in this time of need to protect my precious daughter. I call upon you in my time of need. I need not ask for anything for myself. Just please be here for her this one time." I said.

More blood pooled from my mouth.

"What are you doing? He's not going to answer you. You're a lost soul Lucifer." Said Michael.

Michael was now nearing the bedroom door of Grace. Step by step I heard him make his way down the hallway.

I cleared my throat to the best of my ability.

"Please I ask you these things as a lost soul. But I know my purpose now. Forgive me of all my past. I'm–sorry. I'm sorry for all of it. But most of all Father, please forgive him." I said.

My vision was fading in and out. Everything was turning into pitch white around me.

"Forgive me?" Shouted Michael.

"I–. What's that?" Michael stopped dead in his tracks.

He turned around and stared back at me from down in the hallway, by Grace's door. He let go of the doorknob and backed away. He looked as if he had just seen a ghost. His face was expressionless.

"YES. I UNDERSTAND FATHER. I'm sorry. Yes–I will do as you wish." Said Michael.

"Grac–," I said. Trying to finish her name.

"Grace. You can come out now." Said Michael.

I was confused. Michael approached me, ever so gently. He knelt and whispered into my ear.

"He heard you. He said you're not a mistake. You never were a mistake. It was your duty to be a Father." He whispered.

He cradled me in his lap. His armor was coldly pressed against my cheek.

"I do not question father. And I'm sorry I did this to you. Please forgive me." Said Michael.

My breath was becoming shallow.

"I–forgive–you," I said.

Pitter-patter could be heard from down the hallway. My eyes opened and closed slowly. It was the same pitter-patter noise I had heard, from when I first met my beloved daughter.

"Daddy!" She Shouted.

"I'm sorry child. I thought I was following orders." Said Michael.

Her wings extended touching the walls on her left and right side, and her fists were clenched.

"Screw your orders!" She said angrily.

She fell by my wayside, gripping my hand.

"I can fix you. I can fix this. We just need caffeine. I'll go make some–."

She said before I interrupted her.

"No," I said.

"I ate the fruit. This vessel is finished." I said.

She was still in panic mode. She tried to stop what bleeding she could with a nearby blanket, but it instantly was soaked in blood.

"Not all the way finished." Said Michael.

I stared at him in confusion, as did Grace.

"I have orders to ascend you Lucifer." Said Michael.

I gripped Grace's hand as tight as I could.

"It's–going to be–okay–hunny," I said.

"But what am I supposed to do now? You can't leave me, Dad!" Shouted Grace.

Tears were rolling down her face profusely. She was a mess.

I pointed at her chest, where her heart was. My hand began to tremble.

Two words. Just two words were said.

"Just–love," I said.

My eyes closed. I drew in a breath then I felt as if a calm had been restored to me. Everything was pitch white. I felt as if I was floating, as if I was off the ground flying again. I tried to move but it felt as if I was swimming.

"Lucifer. I know you can't respond to me but I know you can hear me. I'll watch over your daughter. I'll make sure she grows up strong. After all, we are brothers." Said Michael.

I was ascending...

Fourteen Years Later

That was nearly fifteen years ago. My father loved me from the moment he met me to the moment he took his last breath, and for that, I am forever grateful. I've learned how to blend in with mortals over the last fourteen years, probably better than even my Dad. He always was kind of reckless in a sense. Michael trains with me and checks in with me regularly. We even went on our yearly outing where we flew amongst the stars just him and I. I enjoy having my uncle.

But man do I miss you. My heart aches for you even now as I write this letter. Michael said I'm not allowed up there, but the truth is, I need you. They need you.

Lilith grows stronger in power every day. More and more are following her to their doom. I can't fight this battle alone. So I'm coming to find you. It's time for you to come back.

~*Grace*

-**The End**-

About the Author

Tyler Moore has told stories since he was a young man, whether in poetry, short stories, or the very book you are holding now.

He resides in Southeastern, Oklahoma with his three children, wife and numerous dogs and cats.

Read more at www.facebook.com/authortylermoore.

Milton Keynes UK
Ingram Content Group UK Ltd.
UKHW011121050624
443649UK00006B/448